THE TEAC BABY

CHERRY KAY

This is a work of fiction. Similarities to real people, places or events are entirely coincidental.

Copyright 2015 CHERRY KAY

BOOK DESCRIPTION

Ali knew that a one night stand with her attractive history professor was a bad idea and so did he.

With such relationships being forbidden, they both agreed that they would never mention it again and life would carry on like it never happened.

But this is something that is easier said than done for both of them.

Especially when Ali gets the shock of her life and discovers she is pregnant with her teachers baby...

ALSO...

THIS LIMITED EDITION PACKAGE ALSO INCLUDES THE BELOW FREE BONUS BOOK!

The Sheikh's Reluctant Bride

When Sara is photographed in a compromising situation with Sheikh Raphael they both find it awkward.
However, Sheikh Raphael finds it so awkward that he believes the only way to save his honor is by marrying her and telling the world she is his wife.

And Raphael approaches her offering her an obscene amount of money to marry him for a short period of time she finds it hard to say no and she reluctantly agrees.

But she has no idea what she let herself in for...

Table Of Contents

#1 MAIN BOOK – THE TEACHERS BABY

#BONUSBOOK – THE SHEIKH'S RELUCTANT BRIDE

THE TEACHER'S BABY

Chapter One

Four weeks earlier...

I can't believe I got to class on time. Looking around at every full desk in the small room, I spot the only empty seat far in the back. Wonderful, I guess I'll be wearing my ten-year-old glasses today. I don't mind anyway, I definitely want to see the professor clearly. Dr. Gwozdek is famed around the university for being the sexiest teacher on campus. I've never seen him up close, so when I was able to swap into his class at the last minute, earlier this semester, I jumped at the chance. After all, I'd be graduating come summer and I probably would never get the chance again to have him as my teacher.

I squeeze into to the open desk and sit down just in time to watch Professor Gwozdek walk in, always gracing the classroom full of women, and a few guys, with his presence. There seems to be a collective sigh of appreciation.

I pull out my old plastic framed glasses from my dump-me-all bag, held together by tape and prayer alone.

"Good evening everyone, today we'll be finishing up the last of ancient Mesopotamia…" I think all I heard was "good evening." Once I got my glasses on, I was completely distracted by his looks.

If he wanted to, Dr. Gwozdek could quit his job and become the face of Armani. He has angular features, a square jaw, straight nose and masculine chin. His eyes are a smoky blue under thick lashes and an intense brow. His lips are plump and so pink they look temptingly soft.

Dr. G continues to talk to the class, though I don't think anyone is listening, really. This was a bad idea to take this class with this teacher in my final year of college. There was a reason I pushed my history general education requirement back so far. I wasn't any good at it. I mean who likes to sit and memorize a bunch of dates, anyway? Now I have the added challenge of trying to listen to Dr. G, instead of just staring at his expressive hands and lean build, propped casually against his desk at the head of the room.

My overactive imagination is producing a slew of images of the different ways he can pin me to that desk. I take a deep breath and take off my glasses. Really, I only need to listen to his lecture. I don't have to see him. *That's a good solution, great method Ali*…wonderful, now I'm thinking in third person.

"So anyway, enough about what we will be talking about. Let's jump into the lecture." Dr. G's compelling voice breaks through my inner monologue and I start paying attention to the class. "Starting from the back there, I want everyone to tell me something they learned about ancient Mesopotamia."

The class responds with nervous laughter and

comments, no one was prepared for today to be a discussion day. The class falls silent as they wait for the discussion to get started. I glance around and realize everyone is looking at me expectantly.

"Oh, starting with me?" I say in chagrined surprise. Dr. G nods, I wish I could see his expression, but it's probably best that I don't, anyway. I don't want to lose my train of thought while looking at him. "Well I learned that life in Ancient Mesopotamia was about settling for food. There were a lot of farming communities and governments were formed around that, followed by religion and culture until there was full-blown civilizations," I say a bit nervously.

"Why were governments formed in farming communities?" I didn't expect him to follow up with a question; I just hope I don't say anything stupid.

"Because they needed protection, and a way to make sure everyone was fed, I suppose." I answer honestly and Dr. G. nods thoughtfully.

"Very good…what's your name? You aren't usually vocal during discussion, excuse my singling you out."

"My name is Alicia - Ali." Dr. G nods and he moves on to the student in front of me to continue with discussion.

The rest of class goes by quickly since it's pretty much a review day before we move on from Mesopotamia. Dr. G dismisses us thirty minutes early, but most of the class mills around to ask the professor bogus questions, I'm sure. Just so they can remain in his presence and stare a little bit longer.

I don't blame them. I slowly pack up my things to get ready to go. I'm supposed to meet my best friend Kelsey at her place for dinner. She's just returned from a trip abroad to London and we have serious catching up to do. She'll understand if I'm a few minutes late because I just wanted to look at Dr. G a little longer.

I make it to the front of the small room after weaving around closely strewn desks and manage to trip over absolutely nothing once clear of the maze. I drop my bag and what looks like all my life's contents spill onto the floor.

"Whoa, let me help you there." I glance up at Dr. G, who is crouching to help me pick up my things. To say I'm embarrassed that I practically fell in front of him is an understatement, and now he's dangerously close to my spare tampons strewn about on the floor. I glance around and find the classroom empty. There were just a bunch of people milling around…I guess it took me that long to make my way to the front.

"Thanks, you didn't have to." I feel terribly awkward now that I've realized we're the only two left in the room.

"Oh, I don't mind helping out a student. So are you looking forward to the test?" He jokes, trying to make conversation and I try my best not to turn into a complete idiot and communicate normally with him.

"Actually I'm not dreading it. I thought this class would be memorizing a bunch of dates, but I like that it's largely main-idea based, so I think I'll make it." Dr. G looks at me strangely, I think he's feigning hurt, but there is something else in his gaze I can't pinpoint.

"You thought I'd be one of those professors?" He's smirking at me, his plump lips pulled up at the corner, and that little smile melts my insides.

"Well, all of the other history classes I've been forced to take have really colored my perception of history teachers and professors," I answer honestly and try to lighten my comment with a sheepish smile. We manage to get all my things back into my purse and Dr. G straightens quickly. I follow his lead and take a step towards the door.

"So have I changed your perception?" This is the most casual conversation I've ever had with a professor, I must admit. It seems right, almost, that it be with Dr. G.

"I think so…maybe. After all, you're only one history professor in a sea of many." Dr. G nods, his wavy brown hair falling into his face. He runs his fingers through the silky waves, righting it once more. I hadn't noticed it before, but he has great hair. Not too long in the front and short in the back.

"Well I'm glad that I am changing your mind a bit. It's a lifelong battle of mine being a teacher and whatnot." He smiles good-naturedly and I laugh a bit nervously. My goodness, I need to get myself together. I am not some giggling groupie.

"As long as you don't push too many names and dates down my throat then I think we'll be good." I smile at him crookedly and it's his turn to laugh. To say he has a nice laugh is an understatement. It sounds like hot chocolate; warm, seductive and delicious.

"Like I said during class, I don't expect you to memorize dates, but you'll have to remember a few more names, I must admit." There's nice seductive, yet humorous warmth to his voice that makes me feel like the luckiest girl on Earth just to be speaking to him right now.

"Alright, well I guess I won't resent you too much." I smile at him shyly. Cool, I'm doing this, having a normal conversation and not sounding like some star struck student.

"I certainly hope not. I wouldn't want to get on your bad side," he says slowly, his voice deepening a bit. I study his expression; his smoky eyes are intensely focused on me. A warm thrill works its way through my veins.

"No, you could never get on my bad side, Dr. G." He smiles at me crookedly and I catch something unexpected in his gaze. There is definitely a heat there that surprises me.

"Your response in class was very perceptive, why don't you participate during discussions?" Dr. G's voice has become even silkier and all that more seductive. My heart speeds up in a rush of electric excitement, but I'm quick to ignore it. Maybe he's just innately sexy and can't help it if he comes across as a god of seduction.

"Dr. G, so many people jump at the chance for your attention during discussion it's difficult to try and be heard." I say jokingly and he smiles.

"It's okay to call me Adam outside of class Alicia." I try not to show my surprise too much. He wants me to call him by his first name? I can't help but feel a little privileged. Even though I should squash what I'm feeling. He probably tells all of his students this outside of class.

"Okay Adam…it's Ali, actually. Only my parents call me Alicia and that's only if I'm in trouble."

Adam chuckles. "Ali suits you I think." Adam's eyes roam over my face and I bite my lip, his gaze clearly stops at my mouth and locks on. Butterflies take up residence in my belly and my breathing stops short in nervousness.

"Uh, well I have to get going…thanks for helping me with my bag." I take a few steps towards the door and Adam seems to snap out of whatever train of thought he was on. I can almost see the professional friendly demeanor slide firmly back into place.

"Right, no problem Ali, see you next class."

I wave and walk from the room.

I'm definitely confused. Was there something there or wasn't there…? Am I just making things up? That seems most likely as he is my teacher and I have an overactive imagination. Plus, with all the talk of how gorgeous Dr. G is, there have never been rumors about him having any sort of fling with a student before. I sigh and shake my head. Yeah I need to get a grip, and possibly a boyfriend.

I hurry down the hallway and hang a right out to the entrance of the building closest to the parking lot. I walk out into the crisp early winter night air and take a deep breath; I can't wait for the snow to finally get here. The days and nights have been getting cooler and cooler in Connecticut, winding down to the inevitability of snow season. Soon, the sidewalks and paths of the University of Connecticut will be white. It's one of my favorite things about the campus; it looks so good under a blanket of snow.

While getting into my Honda Civic, I dial Kelsey's number, she's sure to be annoyed with me. The girl is honestly a little obsessive when it comes to being on time.

"You should be here by now, I timed the eggplant Parmesan to be ready by the time you got here, and now it's going to be soggy." Kelsey's annoyed breathy voice nags at me through the phone.

"I know, I know. I'm on my way from class now…you won't believe who I had an after class chat with."

Kelsey gasps, her earlier annoyance immediately forgotten. "Oh my gosh! Dr. G, tell me you had Dr. G all to yourself after class!" Kelsey nearly squeals in excitement. "I swear I'm coming to class with you all the time from now on." I laugh at her over excitement.

"Calm down Kels, There isn't even an extra seat in the class, so you'd be sitting on the floor."

Kelsey sighs, long-suffering. "I should have taken world civ all over again instead of the History of English Theater. That professor is a demi god." I roll my eyes, leave it to the theater major to be dramatic.

"Alright, well I just wanted to call to tell you that I'm on the way now. I should be there in five minutes." By now I'm pulling out of university grounds.

"Good, I want to hear every detail about class when you get here, and don't skimp on the imagery, you're a writer, you need to be very descriptive." I laugh and roll my eyes. She's probably going to want me to sneak pictures of Adam next class. I end the call with Kelsey and dial my mom hands-free.

"Oh, is this my daughter Alicia? I was beginning to think I was childless because none of my children ever think to call their mother. I only gave birth to you and make sure you have enough money to eat every week." I smile a little guiltily, but fondly, none the less. She's right; I haven't given her a call in a while. I miss my mom's voice.

"Hi mamma, how are you?"

Shatrice King does her famous sarcastic snort and sighs before telling me she's fine and proceeds to fill me in on the week's events. My dad, Shawn King, got another big client he is defending for a slip and fall suit. Dad is one of the most successful corporate lawyers in Connecticut. A lot of big businesses are on my dad's client list. On the other hand, my mom is a physician's assistant and she always has crazy patient stories to report. My parents are both very successful and though they don't say it outright, there is pressure on my two older brothers and I to be just as successful.

"So that's us, how are you doing in your classes?" I pause before answering her right away, and my ever-perceptive mother catches it instantly. "What's wrong? You didn't fail a test or something, did you?" Her stern voice makes me sigh in mild annoyance; sometimes my mother has too little faith in me, ever since I switched my major from Pre-Med to English.

"No, I haven't failed any tests, mother. My classes are fine; it should be another A plus semester. Anyway, I'm pulling up to Kelsey's now. I'll call later to catch up with daddy." I hurry off the phone with my mom and get out of the car to walk into Kelsey's building and to her apartment.

"Finally!" She greets me in a whirlwind before I so much as knock on her door.

Kelsey is a gorgeous blend of African American and Italian. I often envy her flowing black hair that falls just to her waist. Kels never has to worry about curls that can turn to frizz and ruin everyone's day. She has that soft looking caramel latte skin and her features are perfect and softly rounded. The killers are her eyes; she can get any guy once they've had a look at her forest green eyes. It's what makes her so unique.

"So! Tell me, tell me. Is he as gorgeous up close as he is far away?"

I laugh and pull Kelsey into a fierce hug. "I've missed you! How was England, what did you do, what did you see?"

Kelsey waves away my questions, she's obviously determined. She ushers me to the breakfast bar in the kitchen and starts to make a plate of food for me. "I'll tell you after you spill about class!"

I sigh and give in finally. "Fine, he's gorgeous up close. I mean…obviously he's gorgeous. But it was distracting, trying to listen to him talk and being so close to him at the same time…" I pause for thematic effect and notice Kelsey is staring at me in suspense.

"By God woman, don't stop now!" I laugh, and she grabs a dinner knife, holding it up threateningly.

"Well I dropped my bag after class and he helped me pick up all the stuff, and really we just chatted, but…and this could be my overactive imagination, but I think there was something there…" Hearing myself out loud solidifies my fear that I'm making something out of nothing.

"Were there intense stares? Did he touch you in any way at all?" Kelsey asks with building excitement.

I shake my head. "There was a look and a certain intensity-I don't know. He didn't touch me though. I think it's my imagination."

Kelsey continues fixing my plate and slides it over to me across the breakfast bar. "Well, next class you should definitely have another after-class chat." I roll my eyes and take a bite of the eggplant Parmesan. It's delicious, of course, who doesn't like cheese and sauce covering breaded eggplant.

Kelsey gets her plate and takes a seat next to me. She starts to tell me all about London, but I can't quite focus on what she's saying. All I keep thinking about are smoky blue eyes and a sultry smooth voice.

Chapter 2

The mellow tones of Thievery Corporation stop playing through my headphones and abruptly the ringing sound of my alarm alerts me to the time. Shit, I have ten minutes to get to my evening class. I grab my lesson plans and sweep them into my binder before shoving it into my messenger bag. While slinging the bag across my chest, I hurry out of my office, flipping off the lights as I leave.

I don't even have time to wave to the receptionist of the history department on my way out; I just power through the lobby and opt for using the stairs to the ground floor, taking them two at a time at that. I have to truck all the way across campus so I won't be late for my class. Normally, I would be prepared; normally I'd be five minutes early. Not today, though.

I was purposely trying not to think about my World Civilizations class lately. If I thought about it, then I'd think about her. Alicia, she caught me off guard on the very first day of class. When I chose to start introductions from the back of the class I hadn't realized who was sitting in that seat, all tucked away and hidden like a precious gem. Her looks are what caught me, even though that's something I've learned to put little stock in over the years.

Then last class, when she dropped her things, when I took her in fully and up close, she was sensory overload for me. Her voice was sultry, like a red satin ribbon and she didn't even realize how sexy it was just to hear her talk. She wasn't tall or svelte like other women I've grown accustomed to dating, the modeling type. No, Alicia is average in height and she has all the right curves.

I was beginning to think an hourglass figure was a myth, but not with Ali, her body looked perfect in those form fitting jeans and sweater, which did nothing to cover her up. Then her face, it was smooth and flawless. She has perfect light chocolate brown skin highlighting her light brown eyes perfectly. She has those high cheekbones I know most women would kill for and naturally long lashes under arched eyebrows. Her lips though, they looked so full and inviting. While talking to her, I imagined all the things I could do with those lips…what those lips could do for me.

I shake myself out of this train of thought. This is why I couldn't focus on my lesson plan for the class, Alicia would fill my senses and I'd be hard as a fucking post, my concentration shot to shit. As I weave in and out of foot traffic on the way to the humanities classroom building, I wonder how the hell I'm going to keep my mind focused on my lecture with her in the room.

I all but burst through the doors leading into the classroom building and startle a few students milling around in the lobby. I bypass them and head left down the hall leading to room one-ten. Greeks. I just have to remember that today's class will be about the Hellenistic Mediterranean.

I slow my pace, and check my watch; it's six fifty-nine. I can't believe I made it with a minute to spare. Stopping directly outside the classroom door I take a deep breath, brush my hair out of my face and step into the classroom.

"Good evening everyone, I almost didn't make it on time today." I say, jokingly and glance around the room, my eyes not settling on any one student, I can't deny that I'm looking for her.

Just so I know where not to look for the duration of the class. When my eyes spot her right up front and center I feel like cursing. How does she go from sitting in the back of the class practically all semester to finding a seat in the front row? Maybe she got here earlier today.

I go over to the podium at the head of the room and set my jacket and bag down on the desk and fish out the flash drive with today's presentation on it. Thank goodness I didn't forget it, with how scatterbrained I've been lately. I take a moment to set up the PowerPoint and start the presentation.

There is quiet commotion from the class as they pull out laptops and notebooks. I take the time to watch Alicia move. She has a certain grace to her movements I can't describe. Today her curly black hair is pinned to the side and loose, falling to her upper back. Last class, it was pulled into a tight bun with a few coiled strands falling into her face. She's just so beautiful...I force myself to look away from her and glancing around the room, I see mostly everyone is ready to take notes.

"So today, we're going to be learning about ancient Greece. Then after lecture we'll discuss a recurring theme for why the Greeks were so divided." I manage to get through the lecture portion of class smoothly. I don't forget to mention anything important and I was able to keep my eyes from falling on Alicia entirely.

"Alright, so we have fifteen minutes left for discussion. I want you all to group up into fours and try to come to a consensus for why the Greeks were divided. In about ten minutes we'll get whatever points you all come up with on the board."

The class of twenty-eight students group up into fours a bit awkwardly, rearranging desks and whatnot. I walk around as best I can and facilitate some trains of thought here and there. I make sure to keep away from the group Alicia is in.

Once the ten minutes are up I call the class to attention and ask for what they came up with, hands raise and among them are Alicia's, for once. I choose someone in the back and pull up the projector screen so I can write on the white board behind it.

"So we were talking about how the early Greeks were really invaders of people already settled with their own cultures. There was no mass conquering of land and building of a sort of universal Greek nation."

"Those are great conclusions, and you are absolutely right…what's your name sir?" The student perks up and tells me his name is Destin. "Okay so from Destin and crew, we have pre-existing cultures." I write this on the board in a T chart. "Great point let's expand on this, anyone else?"

The remaining five minutes of class goes well as far as discussion and I wrap everything up feeling satisfied with today's class. A few students remain this time to talk about a few things on the syllabus and the structure of final grades. The usual.

Once the room is emptied, I'm relieved. Alicia didn't drop her things this time. I go to retrieve my flash drive and log out of the computer. When I pull my bag over my shoulder, I notice a pair of heavily taped up glasses on the desk Alicia was occupying…shit. I retrieve them just as she hurries through the classroom door, appearing to be flustered.

"Oh there they are! I thought I dropped them outside somewhere and that they probably got kicked around and were never to be found again."

I smile at her politely. "Well these are clearly fighters. I don't think you can get rid of them so easily." She laughs and the sound has some sort of direct link to my cock, which stiffens in reaction.

"Yeah they are fighters for sure. I think now of days that faith alone keeps them together." She says silkily, I realize belatedly that I'm still holding on to her glasses and hand them to her.

She reaches out and her fingers brush over mine. The

brief contact of her smooth skin sends my mind into a conflict. I want to touch her, more of her. That was too brief, it wasn't enough.

"So did you enjoy today's class, Alicia?" Shit, my voice is too husky. I clear my throat and she tilts her head at me, smiling adorably. Another thing about her was her smile. She had the deepest dimples in both cheeks.

"I thought I told you to call me Ali. It sounds weird when you use my whole name." She captures the corner of her plump bottom lip between her teeth and my mind wanders to her mouth again. Shit I can't do this…this isn't right, to think about a student like this. But fuck me if all I can think about are her delicious lips clamped firmly around my hardening cock right now.

"Right, I'm sorry…so did you enjoy lecture, Ali?" My voice is betraying my train of thought and her eyes are clouding with bemusement.

"I did, I like Greek and Roman history…I really enjoyed the discussion, even though you didn't spot my hand up when I wanted to input." Her voice is small and I study her expression.

"What's wrong?" It was taking everything in me to keep my hands and feet firmly planted where they were. All I want to do is pull her tight against me and taste her lips on mine.

"It's nothing, I'm probably being silly, but it felt like

you were ignoring me or something." She tries to cover up her concern with nonchalance and I curse myself. Now I've hurt her feelings, in a small way yes, but that's the last thing I want to do, I'm not a selfish or mean guy, and I was today. Ali has turned me inside out in less time than it takes to tie a shoe.

"I...I didn't mean to ignore you, Ali. Do you still have something to say about lecture? You have me all to yourself now." I smile at her and she gazes up at me through lowered lashes. The sexiest look crosses over her features, and she is still biting her fucking lip.

"I have you all to myself? Or do you mean you don't have any more classes for the night." She speaks as if she's trying to convince herself that I didn't just say something so inappropriate.

"I mean I'm all ears and no I don't have any classes after this one." Ali brushes her hair from her face and takes a breath.

"Well, all I wanted to say was covered I guess...about the Greeks being divided largely because Greece is made up of many islands in the Aegean. So there were different island nations...and yeah that's all I wanted to get off my chest." I can't help but laugh, she's being so cute.

"Very good, I'm glad you're enjoying this topic and really grasping the main ideas." Ali nods once, smiling.

"Yeah I am, so far no dates to memorize so we're good." She takes a casual step towards the closed door to leave and I surprise her as well as myself by reaching out to grab her hand. She holds her breath out of surprise, more than anything else and looks down at my hand. "Is there something you need…?" Her voice has gone breathless and I curse myself for acting so impulsively, but I can't deny that I just wanted to touch her.

"No. Yes…I don't know Ali, I just want…you." Her breathing speeds up and she takes two steps towards me.

Shit, shit, shit…this shouldn't be happening. But fuck, if I'll stop whatever is about to start. Ali stops moving when she's a breath away from me, her hand twisting in mine to break free and find its way to my chest. I grip her waist with both of my hands and pull her firmly against me. My cock presses against her belly and she gasps just in time for me to press my mouth to hers, licking in between her parted lips to taste the sweetness of her tongue.

She melts into me with a low moan and my hands slip from her waist to grip the fullness of her sexy ass. She moans in surprise and honestly, I'm just as floored as to what's happening as she is. I hold her against me even tighter and grind my erection against her. Ali's hands feverishly un-tuck my shirt and her hands slip underneath it to splay across my back.

The contact of her hands on my skin sends me into a sort of frenzy. I want more of her against my skin, now. I pull her bag from her shoulder and push off her jacket. I back her up against the board, out of sight from the small window in the door, not that anyone would be in this building this late. Sliding my hands underneath her sweater I pull it off in one smooth motion.

"Shit baby, lace?" She really was created just to bring me to my knees. I cup her lace-covered breasts and simply devour them. I lick and suck on the inviting cusps and pull one nipple into my mouth through the lace, my tongue flicking against it and running around it in circles. Ali's gasps and moans only fuel my burning desire for her. What's coursing through every one of my veins is all consuming and I couldn't stop now if I tried. I reach around her back and unclasp her bra in one swift motion. The fabric falls from her skin and she's bared to me.

"Oh my god." Her voice is ten times sexier when toned with lust, even when she sounds as if she can't believe this is happening.

"I know, but please don't tell me to stop now." I study her face, her eyes are heated and thankfully she shakes her head, wanting me to continue. I massage her breasts with my hands and then suck her other nipple into my mouth and bite down gently. Ali cries out and my cock jumps painfully at the sound. Her hands are in my hair, holding me against her skin. I know she wants this just as much as I do.

I lick and suck my way down to her hips, getting on my knees as I undo her jeans and pull them down slowly. She smells so good, almost like caramel, it's heady. I kiss her thigh and continue pulling her jeans off. I free her ankles of the jeans and look up at her while I hook my fingers into her matching lacy panties and pull them off. Her chest is rising and falling rapidly with each pant and the sight of her… beautifully naked with her flawless light chocolate skin. Her nipples beg for attention as the darker tightly peaked nubs call for my mouth.

"You're so beautiful, Alicia." I whisper almost reverently and her hooded eyes meet mine and lock on. I can't quite read what she's thinking in her heated gaze, but I know that she's as caught up in whatever rocket science is happening between us as I am. Ali bites her lip and I groan. I stand up and pass my tongue across her bottom lip before taking it in between my teeth. Her lips are softer than I could ever imagine.

Her hands are on me, unbuttoning my shirt and pulling my belt from my pants. She unbuckles my slacks and pushes them down until I can step out of them and I shrug off my shirt. Her hands run all over my chest, my stomach, and my back. Each caress feels like a lick from a fire goddess. She slides her hand past the waistband of my boxers and grips me in her hand firmly, stroking it up and down slowly, torturously.

"Fuck, Alicia…" I groan and she pushes me back against the desk. I watch as she pulls my boxers off and kneels down, her mouth dangerously close to my cock. "Don't tease me, don't tease…" Ali glances up at me, I can feel her breath on my shaft. I'm dangerously close to losing it and coming all over her face, all she has to do is put her mouth on me. Something I've imagined six different ways already.

"I would never tease you Dr. G…is this what you want?" She flicks her tongue out against the head of my cock and circles it around before sucking me into her mouth. That coupled with the fact that she called me Dr. G in that sexy ass voice has me pushing my fingers into her hair and pushing myself into her mouth.

She takes me so deep; I can feel her swallow around the sensitive head. I curse loudly and spurt into her mouth with a dizzying orgasm. She takes everything and sucks me clean. I simply stare at her in awe.

"You're so sexy, Ali, you're so fucking sexy." I chant while pulling her up and bending her over onto the desk. I lean down along her back so I can whisper in her ear. "You're going to be the sexiest fantasy I've ever had come true." I feel her shiver and I straighten. Her ass is glorious, sticking out just for me to smack and I do. Ali cries out, followed by a moan and I do it again.

"Please Adam…please I need you inside." I spread her cheeks and guide my still hard cock into her perfectly tight, warm and silky core.

"Ah…fuck baby, your pussy is heaven." Ali moans at my heated words and pushes back onto me so that I slide deeper inside of her. She's so tight. This is going to be over fast if I don't pace myself. I push deep, drawing out a breathless moan from her and retreat. I plan to stroke her slowly, but she has other ideas and pushes back onto me, increasing the pace.

Her beautiful behind jiggles with every drive into her. I grip her waist and thrust hard and she clenches around me so tightly, causing me to groan. I stand on the tips of my toes to get a better angle and she becomes even more vocal.

Ali's cries of pleasure fill my ears and soon all I know is her. "Adam please, harder…" she begs breathlessly. I give her everything she wants, shit, at this point I'd give her the moon if she wants it.

"Come for me, Ali." I beg and, as if on command, I feel her tighten and spasm around me, massaging my cock and milking another orgasm from me. She cries out in ecstasy and I call out her name in kind as I pound my release into her. We both fly off the edge of heaven in absolute pleasure.

Then that moment of clarity, when all the lust and heat you feel no longer clouds your mind, descends onto me. I just…I just had sex with Ali in the classroom…on my desk. Without a condom. Shit.

"Ali…tell me you're on birth control." I slide out of her and she slowly stands up she has such a beautiful afterglow, her features are calm, she's sated and very much a satisfied female.

"Yeah I'm on the pill," she says without concern and

I relax tremendously.

"Good...good." Ali leans into me and stretches up to kiss me. Her lips are tender and the strangest feeling of warmth invades my chest.

"You don't...do you do this...often?" Her eyes are unsure now as she takes in our clothing strewn about the classroom. Of course she'd think I have sex with students often with how I just took her without much preamble. I walk over to my bag and retrieve some tissues. I pull Ali in front of me and gently push her legs open a bit to clean her up.

"I think my lack of preparation with a condom is self-explanatory."

"So you're...single?" She says this so hopefully, I can't help but chuckle.

"Yes I'm single Ali, are you?" I ask and she nods. "Well, now that we have that awkward conversation out of the way...do you maybe want to get something to eat with me?" Ali tilts her head at me and bursts into laughter.

"This is so backwards, but yeah I'd love to." I don't know what's driving my attachment to her, and even though I've had her, I still want more.

We silently get dressed and she makes sure to put her glasses in her purse. We leave the classroom and I flip off the lights on the way out. I know her mind is working at a million miles per hour as we walk down the hallway in contemplative silence.

"What are you thinking, Ali?" I ask, as I hold the door open for her while exiting the building.

"This is just all a little…incredible to me." She answers honestly and I study her face as she studies mine intently.

"Trust me, I can't rationalize much either…I just know that I want you." I answer honestly, more honest than I've ever been with a woman before.

Chapter Three

All of what just happened was impossible to believe. I just had amazing sex with a professor. Not with any old professor either, Dr. G. If someone would've told me this morning that I'd end up bent over his desk like I was, I'd tell them they were out of their minds. I mean he's a professor for Christ's sake! Shouldn't this be wrong? It doesn't feel wrong, though. I loved every second of it and I don't feel guilty. Adam is gorgeous, sure he's a little older than me, but honestly he looks like he's still in his twenties and he wants me. He said so himself and that has to mean something.

"Where did you park?" Adam asks as we make our way towards the parking lot.

"Just a few rows back there." I point in the general direction of my car and Adam nods.

"Alright, do you mind giving me a lift to my car? Then we can meet up at…The Pelican for seafood?"

"Yeah, of course and seafood sounds great." I smile at him a bit shyly. What could we possibly talk about now? "How old are you?" The question jumps out of my mouth without my approving it first.

"I'm thirty-three…does that bother you?"

I shake my head. "No I was just curious…I'm twenty-one. I guess you could've figured that out since I'm a senior and all." We reach my car and I unlock the doors for us to climb in.

"Yeah, I figured you were around there somewhere. I've never… 'dated' someone so much younger than me before." I wonder if he feels guilty about what we did and the fact that I'm his student.

"Do you regret it?" Another question that jumps out without permission. I'm tense in waiting for him to answer. I haven't pulled out of the parking spot yet; we're just sitting silently in the car.

"I don't want to lie to you…I just don't know yet."

I take a deep breath and ask him where his car is; he's parked it in the North Parking Garage. The short car ride is quiet and I wonder if dinner is going to be painfully awkward. I should've never asked him that question. I pull up behind his shiny black Audi and he gets out of the car, but before he closes the door he leans inside.

"Do you know how to get to The Pelican?" I nod and then he closes my car door and gets into his.

I pull away and head to the restaurant, glancing every so often in my rear view mirror to make sure he was following me, that he didn't ditch me. I pull into the parking lot of The Pelican and find a spot pretty close to the entrance. I decide to wait outside for Adam; he walks up a minute later, his eyes trained on me, he is just so intense.

"Shall we?" He takes my hand and I smile widely, he

has such an innate way of making a girl feel special.

We walk into the elegantly rustic restaurant and I can't help but notice how easily he draws attention. Women's heads turn from every direction to look at him; I kind of love that he's holding my hand now.

"Party for two?" The host, dressed in all black, smiles politely at us and Adam nods his head. "Great, if you'll follow me."

The host leads us towards the back of the restaurant. Near the kitchen, is a secluded booth. He sets two menus down on the table and promises our waiter will be by shortly. I slide into the booth; the plush red leather is comfortable and cozy. Adam sits across from me and I pick up the menu, perusing the options. I soon notice Adam staring at me rather than reading his menu.

"What?" I ask, smiling at him in question.

Adam pushes his fingers through that soft wavy hair and I remember how silky it felt. "Nothing...I just like looking at you, you're so beautiful." I bite my lip, a little embarrassed. No one has ever pointed that out so plainly.

"Thank you. You aren't so bad to look at either, you know."

Adam snorts sarcastically, it sounds eerily like my mother's sarcastic snort. "I wish that weren't the case sometimes. Especially with my being a teacher."

Adam presses his lips together as if he wished he didn't mention that.

"You know, you can't leave me guessing tonight. What possessed you to…come on to me?" I ask a bit awkwardly, not wanting to ask my real question, why he decided to have sex with me, out loud in public.

Adam sighs and is about to reply when our waiter comes by the table. He's tall and handsome in a boy next-door kind of way, with a cool haircut and green eyes that plays off his caramel colored skin almost strikingly.

"Hello folks, my name is Trey and I'll be your server for tonight. Can I start you off with something to drink?" I order plain lemonade and Adam orders water. The waiter nods and he glances at me with a double take. "I'm sorry, I feel like we've met before…do you go to UConn?" I blink at him in surprise, though I can't place him. I don't think I'd forget a face like his.

"Yeah I do…I'm sorry I can't remember where I've seen you before." I smile apologetically and Trey shrugs nonchalantly.

"It's all good, we met at a poetry slam one night. I don't think you would remember me though, because you were pretty much in a rush when I tried to introduce myself."

"Oh, I'm sorry. Well, it's nice to meet you, Trey." I smile and Trey is about to say something when Adam cuts him off.

"Sorry man, but I really need that water." I'm a little surprised that Adam interrupted so bluntly, almost rudely. Trey apologizes and hurries to get what we ordered. I look at Adam expectantly and he shrugs.

"He was clearly flirting." Adam says it simply as if that explains everything. Since we're so close to the kitchen, Trey comes back with our drinks in no time.

"Here y'all are. Have you had a chance yet to go over the menus?"

"We haven't." Adam answers curtly and Trey says he'll give us a few minutes to look it over. I glance at my menu and decide the fish and chips are my best bet.

"So why don't you have a boyfriend?" Adam asks me almost casually, though he's looking at me intently.

"I never really had anyone pursue me, I guess." Adam quirks an eyebrow at me.

"The waiter doesn't count?"

I laugh and then shrug. "I guess sometimes I'm oblivious to advances…" Adam shifts in his seat and he takes a drink of his water. I watch his neck move while he works the liquid down his throat. Everything he does is captivating; it's not natural.

"I guess I did well then in catching your attention." Adam quirks an eyebrow at me with a mischievous grin and I giggle.

"Yeah I guess so."

Dinner with Adam goes well. Trey eventually gets the message and stops trying to flirt with me. Adam and I don't discuss the whole, "he's a teacher, I'm his student" thing and we talk about regular stuff like our interests, aspirations, hobbies, favorite movies and shows. Adam is just as interesting as his looks. He wants to someday teach at Yale and plays amateur hockey as a pastime. He loves old nineties sitcoms, which I'm a big fan of The Nanny and Friends, myself. I wanted to kiss him when he said he loves Pixar films.

"Adam, my favorite movie of all time is Finding Nemo."

His eyes widen, as does his grin. "No way, I could recite to you every line of that movie." I laugh and Trey returns with Adam's receipt after he paid the check.

We head outside and Adam walks me the few steps to my car. "I don't really want tonight with you to end," he admits and I look at him in surprise, his smoky blue eyes are sincere, he's serious.

"I have Finding Nemo in HD back at my apartment…if you want to watch?" Adam smiles seductively and he leans forward to kiss me on the cheek.

"I'll follow you." I nod and watch him walk across the parking lot to his car. I take a deep breath and hurry into my car to lead the way home. Once we reach my building, I tell him to park in my guest spot. And wait for him in the lobby. My parents didn't want me in any sort of student housing, they said I'd be too distracted by college parties and student "antics." . So my dad pays for my apartment just a fifteen-minute drive away from campus.

"This is a nice looking building for a student salary," Adam says as he walks into the lobby.

"My scholarships pay for most of the bills, it's not too bad." Adam nods, seemingly impressed by my answer.

We walk over to the elevator and ride up to the fourth floor, three other people accompany us on the elevator and the two women in the car can't keep from sending him furtive glances. I want to mark him as mine in some way, tell the world that we have something going. I lead Adam down to my front door once we are off the elevator and we step inside.

Thank goodness, I live alone because as soon as the door shuts, Adam's hands are gripping my waist and his mouth is on my neck as he pushes me back against the wall.

"We can save Nemo for later," he whispers huskily as his fingers slide past my jeans and panties and into my sensitive folds. Why would I argue with his logic?

The night is filled with Adam and he could never get enough. I fall asleep exhausted against his warm chest with his arms encircled around me.

Waking up feeling extremely relaxed and sated, I couldn't deny I was happy. Not to mention warm, Adam is draped over me like a blanket. His hand is cupping one of my breasts and his other arm encircles my waist while his legs tangle with mine. I check the clock on my bedside table, it's almost noon and I have a class in two hours. It's past the time to get out of bed. I try to gingerly extract myself from Adam without waking him, but as soon as I remove his hand from my boob, he stirs.

"What time is it?" He asks, his voice thick and groggy. I turn around in his arms and smile shyly.

"It's almost noon."

He blinks at me a couple of times until what I said sinks in, and then he panics. "Shit! I missed a class." He jumps up and scrambles for his things, dressing quickly and searching for his car keys.

"Will you get in trouble?" I ask teasingly, trying to lighten his mood, but he just keeps looking for his car keys in his bag. He finds them and rakes his hair back while taking a deep breath.

"No, but I don't want a bad reputation."

I almost laugh. "I don't think you could ever have a bad reputation." Adam's eyes roam across my face, he's thinking about something, but I can't quite tell what it is when he's being so serious. "Will I see you today?" I ask innocently enough and his eyebrows come together, his expression reluctant, almost. I tilt my head at him, what's with the sudden change?

"We should probably get together…I mean talk-during my office hours today. Can you meet me at around four?" I nod slowly and Adam slings his bag across his chest. "I'll see you then." Without so much as another glance, he walks from my room and soon I hear the front door open and close.

This feels all wrong…I need to tell Kelsey about all of this, she'll help me put it into perspective. I don't want to invest my emotions into whatever is between Adam and I when nothing can happen between us. I grab my cell phone from the nightstand and dial Kelsey.

"Hey girl, are you on campus? Do you want to get some lunch with me?" Hearing Kelsey's voice is calming. I probably shouldn't tell her everything over the phone, though.

"Kelsey, come over…it's important." At the serious tone of my voice, all talk of lunch stops.

"Of course, I'm on my way, can you give me something over the phone?" I chew on my lip a moment and then sigh.

"It's about Adam…" There's a pause and I sigh again. "Dr. G…" Kelsey gasps dramatically and I roll my eyes.

"I'm on the way, I'm freaking out at the implications of your calling him Adam, but I'm on the way." Kelsey hangs up and I take the time to gingerly get out of bed and shower, I haven't had sex in a while and I'm feeling particularly tender.

My apartment is great in that it has all the modern amenities, especially the glass enclosed shower with rainfall showerhead. It's often my go-to place to de-stress. Today is the first day that it isn't working to soothe my nerves. After my shower, I brush my teeth at the sink and run moisturizer through my hair so I can detangle it. I think I'll just pull it into a ponytail today.

Just as I'm getting dressed in warm tights and a sweater dress, I hear a knock on the door. I hurry to open it and Kelsey barrels inside.

"Tell me everything," she demands while pulling me into the living room and down onto the couch.

"We…we had sex…several times." Kelsey's jaw drops and she stares at me as if I have three heads made of gold.

"You lucky bitch." Is the first thing out of her mouth. I would normally laugh, but honestly I'm too confused for our usual banter. Kelsey realizes that I'm not myself and she takes my hand. "So what happened?" I tell her everything and by the end of the story, she's pacing back and forth around the living room.

"It doesn't make any sense. It sounds like he was being really sweet and truthful before and now he wants to have a meeting during his office hours? Maybe he lied, Ali…maybe he really does have a lot of affairs with students and just dodged your question. He treated you like any girl would want to be treated so he could have a good time." Kelsey's words hurt, but I couldn't deny her logic. He didn't actually answer my question when I asked him if he did this a lot.

My hope in Adam is quickly fading away. Kelsey is right, there's no way she can't be.

"He's gonna tell me we can't see each other anymore then." I say quietly. Kelsey sits down on the couch and hugs me tightly. I simply sigh and hug her back. "It was too good to be true, I guess." I murmur and Kelsey pulls away a fraction, her hands gripping my shoulders.

"Ali, from hearing about all this sex you were having…did you guys use protection?" I press my lips together guiltily and Kelsey groans forebodingly. "You know you're my best friend, my soul mate, but Alicia that was stupid." She says bluntly and I bite my lip in consternation.

It was stupid, especially as Adam wasn't up front with me about his sex life. "We need to get you checked out ASAP." Kelsey grabs her cell phone and hands it to me. We use the same gynecologist and the doctor's office number is saved in her contacts.

"Go ahead and make the appointment." I sigh and stand up to walk out onto the balcony off the living room and make the call.

*

I know what he's going to say, I'm his student and he's my professor. We can't have any sort of fling. God forbid something bad happens and the university finds out? He can kiss his aspirations of teaching at Yale goodbye.

It was dumb of me to think something could happen. I'm about to graduate and I need to focus on that and my career, anyway. I walk into the history building and take the elevator up to the teachers' wing. I push open the glass doors to the reception area and tell the older woman at the desk that I'm here to see Dr. G. She picks up the phone and dials a single digit on the keypad.

"Adam, there's a student here to see you, an Alicia King." The receptionist alerts him to my arrival and she nods once before hanging up the phone. "You can go on back, dear."

I take a deep breath and head to the right, down the long office lined hallway. I reach room three nineteen and push open the door without bothering to knock. My expression is carefully blank and I try not to let myself display any of the upset I'm feeling. I can't deny I'm disappointed and a little hurt. Also, I can't help but beat myself up for being so stupidly naïve in thinking we could have some sort of relationship.

"Please close the door." Is the first thing he says to me, his tone detached and professional. I step back and push the door closed with one finger before taking a seat in one of the chairs on the other side of his fancy looking mahogany desk. He is wearing a blue sweater, the color of his eyes, which clings to his defined chest and arms. I take a minute to control my reaction to him; it's frustrating that I still want him.

"I'm sure you have an idea of why I wanted to talk to you today."

"I do…I guess I understand that you don't want to be involved with me." I answer simply and he almost shakes his head.

"Because of school policy I don't think it wise to risk having any sort of romantic relationship, Alicia." My eyes flit to the wide window behind him, it looks out onto the Great Lawn. Students can be seen lounging in the grass, even though it's colder they still bundle up and find comfortable spots there to study.

"School policy…right. Well I understand…I guess." I mumble and shift in the seat; I just want to leave already.

"I'm sorry, but I shouldn't have let anything happen last night. I just don't want to jeopardize either your future or mine." I nod, and glance around the room. I can't look at him, if I do I'll probably beg him to reconsider, so this is best.

"I understand where you're coming from and I don't blame you…it was a two way street." I try to sound understanding, but keep my expression schooled into careful blankness. I can't let him see that he's affected me way more than I've affected him…if I did at all. That is probably least likely as he's handling this so professionally, it seems almost practiced; another marker that he probably has many affairs with students and gives them this same speech afterward.

"Thank you for being so understanding Ali…I don't know what else to say other than I'm sorry." He finishes lamely and I stand up with my bag.

"I don't need your apology Dr. G. I'll see you tomorrow in class," I say crisply and promptly leave the room, all but running out of the building.

Great, now how was I supposed to survive the remainder of the semester? Soon finals will be coming up and so far I just don't want to go to this man's class and have to see his face every other night. I take a deep breath once I'm outside in the cool fresh air, my phone vibrates in my bag and I fish it out. It's Kelsey.

"Hey." I say and make my way towards the Student Union. I'm feeling for some Panda Express. Their Crab Rangoon always does a good job of lifting my spirits.

"How did it go?" she asks tentatively and I sigh deeply.

"Like we expected. He's a professor, I'm a student and there are 'school policies.'" I say sarcastically.

"I'm sorry, babe. You're sleeping over at my place tonight and we're going to gain a few pounds from ice cream and pizza." I smile. Its times like this when I really love Kelsey.

"Thanks, I need it. I just don't know how the hell I'm supposed to go to his class from now on," I admit and Kelsey sighs.

"You just have to power through it. Don't make eye contact with him, ever, and I think you can deal..." Kelsey trails off and I can almost hear her thinking. "So when is your doctor's appointment? You are on birth control, right?" Kelsey asks gently, though I know she's really worried.

"It's in like ten days, on November 13th and yes I am, don't worry." Kelsey breathes a sigh of relief and I tell her that I'll call a little later. It's always loud in the Student Union and I'd never be able to carry a phone conversation inside.

While waiting in line at Panda Express, I get a text message from one of my older brothers, Trenton, who has been away in California, busy with his new job at Google. He's coming home this weekend and is looking forward to seeing me. If Trent is coming home, then his twin brother Tristan is bound to surprise us with a visit from D.C. Tristan is currently on the White House staff as an intern, he has big dreams of one day holding a seat in the United Nations.

Wonderful, mom and dad's precious Pride and Joy will be at Sunday dinner. Just what I need, looks and double talk from both parents urging me to be more like my brothers and "do something with my life." Just because I am majoring in English doesn't mean I'm throwing away my future.

It's finally my turn to order at Panda Express and I make sure I get Crab Rangoon in my to-go I hide out in the library for the rest of the day, studying for tests I have in both Psych classes that I'm taking for my minor. Once six-thirty comes around, I leave campus to go straight to Kelsey's. I don't even want to stop by my place to pick up clothes; Adam left his imprint all over my apartment.

I knock on Kelsey's door and she opens up, she looks ready for pizza and ice cream, wearing sweat pants and a tank top. She pulls me inside for a hug and shuts the door behind me.

"I've picked up the ice cream, cookie and brownie dough combo of course, and the pizza will be here soon." I follow Kelsey through her open concept apartment and into her bedroom where she finds me something comfortable to wear. She hands me an oversized long sleeved shirt, and I change in her giant walk-in closet. Swapping my dress for the shirt and my boots for plain socks.

"So I didn't ask you earlier but, did you ask him if he had affairs with other students or what?" Kelsey asks when I join her in the living room. She has Netflix ready on stand-by on the flat screen.

"No I didn't ask…I think deep down I was afraid to. My appointment is in less than two weeks anyway and I really don't think he has any STI's." Kelsey sits back on the couch and she hands me a spoon before picking up the big tub of cookie and brownie dough ice cream.

"So Thirteen Going on Thirty or a Gilmore Girls marathon?" Kelsey asks and I opt for Gilmore Girls. That show is just on point sometimes. If I were an actress I'd want to be Alexis Bledel…the more ethnic version, of course.

"So my brothers are coming for Sunday dinner this weekend," I mention to Kelsey as we watch the show and are waiting for the pizza to get here.

"I've got nothing to do this weekend, I can come with you if you want."

I nod fervently. "Yes please." I beg and Kelsey laughs.

"Don't worry, I got your back. Anyway you'll be able to prove your parents wrong when you write that NY Times best seller, make millions and open your own family psych practice." I smile and take a spoonful of cookie dough.

"Got that right." I grin and relax some for the first time in what feels like forever.

***

Today is D-day, the day I go to the GYN's office and I'm not looking forward to it. Kelsey asks me if I want her there. I wonder why she's so adamant about my appointment and what I may or may not find out when I go. I promise her I'd be fine on my own.

To say I get nervous when going to any sort of doctor's office is an understatement. When I was five, I dislocated my elbow on a bad fall at the playground and my mom took me to the hospital where she worked. All the poking and prodding and examining just didn't sit right with me as a kid and ever since then I hated having to go to the doctor.

Walking into the sterile reception area, I go up to the sign-in window and write my name and appointment time on the clipboard. The nurse sitting behind the window smiles at me warmly and tells me to have a seat and wait for my name to be called. I find an empty chair next to an end table with magazines on it and pretend to read one about women's health. The room is not necessarily full, but there is a good amount of women waiting to be seen by a doctor. A few look unconcerned and others exhibit nervous movements. A tapping of the foot, or drumming of the fingers. I think I fall in the waiting nervously category. I'm not looking forward to the doctor poking around my most private area.

"Alicia King." A nurse steps out of the door leading back to the examining rooms. I place the magazine where I found it and stand up to go and get this over with. The nurse looks friendly enough, her badge reads: Kylie Brown, she's dressed in baby pink scrubs and white Keds. Her platinum blonde hair is pulled back into a tight ponytail and her features are beautifully sun kissed. I bet she has never had to get an STI screening.

"Just this way into room two." I walk ahead of her and into the examination room. "I just need to get your weight and a few vital signs." I put my bag down and step on the scale placed against the wall next to the door.

After the nurse jots down my weight she tells me to sit down on one of the chairs in the room and she takes my pulse and blood pressure. "Your heart rate is a little high, are you nervous?" She asks soothingly, trying to make me feel a little more comfortable.

"Yeah a little, I don't really like doctor's offices." I say it sheepishly and she smiles at me apologetically.

"Don't worry Dr. Wilson is great. So you're here for a general checkup and full screening?" I nod once and the nurse walks across the room to a set of cabinets and drawers facing the daunting examination bed. She pulls out a white paper gown and tells me to undress and put it on before the doctor comes in. The nurse gives me an encouraging smile before leaving to give me some privacy.

Taking a deep breath, I get undressed and drape my clothes on the chair with my bag and then sit up on the examination bed. Soon after, there are two swift raps against the wooden door and Dr. Wilson walks in. She is a tall white woman with handsome features, greying black hair, and dark brown eyes.

"Hello Alicia, it's been a while since I've seen you here. How are you?" She asks warmly and I offer a small smile.

"I've been okay, focused on school, really." Dr. Wilson nods as she washes her hands in the sink and dries them with a paper towel.

"That's always good to hear. So you're here today for a full screening, correct?" I nod once and her eyes lock with mine. "I'm going to throw in a pregnancy test just for the heck of it, I know you're on birth control, but it can't hurt to be one hundred percent sure about things. Can I assume you've had unprotected sex recently?" I nod once again, felling mortified that I'm even here for that reason. "Alright, don't worry, most of these tests have quick result turn-around and if there's anything, we'll call you to let you know."

"Okay." I sigh and Dr. Wilson instructs me to lie back so she can begin her exam.

About fifteen minutes later I'm dressed, anxious, and heading back to my car. I hope they don't call me. I hope they have absolutely no reason to call me that they actually feel it's necessary to lose my number altogether. That would be ideal. Never do I want to go through this stress ever again. I'm not having sex again until I'm married and I know my husband is clean. I remove the Band-Aid from my arm; the doctor wanted to be thorough and took samples of my blood for several tests.

I sit in the car and fiddle with the Band-Aid, at a bit of a loss for what to do next. I have an exam coming up in World Civ and I've been really slacking with that class. I should take the day to study; I can't afford to fail the last test before finals. Dr. G hasn't so much as acknowledged my existence in the class and I managed to convince myself that I was fine with it, that things were better that way.

I start the car and buckle my seatbelt before heading to campus to go and study the hell out of all things Hellenistic Era. Kelsey calls me while I'm on the way to the library. I try and hurry my pace so I can get into the building already. There's a freezing cold wind that seems to be determined to turn me into an icicle as I make my way from the parking garage.

I answer Kelsey's call and she asks me about my GYN appointment right off the bat. "So how did it go? Are you clean?" I sigh and roll my eyes at her dramatically urgent tone.

"You better be alone, asking those questions out loud and all. Yes as far as the doctor could tell, I'm fine, but I won't know for sure until the lab results come in." I tell her what I learned from Dr. Wilson so far and Kelsey lets out a small sigh of relief.

"Good. Well I just wanted to make sure you were okay." I brush off Kelsey's concern, not wanting to admit just yet how I really am a little freaked out that I had to go through this entire ordeal.

"Yes, I'm fine, no worries. I'm headed into the library now, I'll talk to you a little later?" Kelsey lets me go and I hurry into the library, not looking in front of me as I'm focused on getting out of the cold. Of course I nearly plow right into Dr. G.

"Sheesh, are you okay?" He asks in concern with an undertone of annoyance. He's holding onto my elbows as I try to regain balance. I don't think he's realized it's me yet. I look up at his painfully gorgeous face and his eyes cloud over with several different emotions. "Alicia..." He says, trailing off awkwardly.

"I am so sorry, I wasn't looking..." I say to fill in the silence. Dr. G. lets me go abruptly and takes a step back.

"It's alright, honestly, I wasn't watching my step either. I'm late for a family dinner." He says in a choppy explanation. I nod and force myself to look away from his smoky gaze.

"Oh-well...sorry for bumping into you...enjoy your dinner." I reply just as awkwardly and quickly retreat into the library.

Great, just great. That's exactly what I need right now, how was I going to focus on studying for his class now? I remember Kelsey's advice and simply resolve to power through it. I wouldn't let him throw me off track anymore. With that in mind, I successfully manage to study for the test and make it through his class the next day without feeling awkward at all.

Soon, the semester will be over and with the coming of winter break, I can forget about Adam all together. I walk into my apartment and collapse onto the couch. Kelsey wants me to come over to her place so I can hang out with her and some guys she is in a study group with. Kelsey has been trying to set me up lately, probably trying to get my mind off of Dr. G, but I'm just not up to it tonight. I fish my phone out of my pants pocket to text her and I see I have a call coming from Dr. Wilson's office.

With my heart hammering in my chest I tap the answer icon. "Hello?"

"Hello Alicia, this is Dr. Wilson." Dr. Wilson's almost motherly voice sounds through the receiver and I swallow past the feeling of doom that's sneaking its way around my neck.

"Hi Dr. Wilson…" I reply, trailing off expectantly so she can just tell me what it is, no beating around the bush.

"I'm calling to inform you of a…result we just got back from the lab concerning your pregnancy test. Well, it came back positive, it read that you are just about two weeks pregnant. All your other tests came back negative, which is great. So I wanted to refer you to a colleague of mine who is an OB-GYN, Dr. Cassidy, she is a very good obstetrician and I think you'll be in good hands with her.

I've already sent over your chart and set up an appointment for you with her for next week, on Tuesday. Her office will be in touch with you to confirm. Now I know you are on birth control, but these things happen, though they are rare. You'll need to stop taking your birth control pills immediately and I'd recommend starting pre-natal vitamins…do you have any questions for me?" She asks softly and I simply stare off into space, my eyes wide and glazed over from shock.

"I'm…are you sure I'm pregnant?" I ask and I can hear the rustling of papers in the background on her end.

"Yes, we actually run all pregnancy tests twice just to be sure. You came back positive both times." I swallow past the lump in my throat and grasp for something, anything else that would make this not true, or a mistake.

"But I'm on birth control…I don't understand how that could happen." I reply and Dr. Wilson sighs, sadly almost.

"I know it's shocking and a lot to take in, but contraception is never one hundred percent effective, Ali." She says apologetically. "Dr. Cassidy is a great obstetrician, like I've said, and she can answer any and all questions you have about the pregnancy when you see her on Tuesday." Dr. Wilson is already washing her hands of me, passing me onto an…obstetrician. Because I'm pregnant…I'm pregnant, with a child growing inside of me.

"Thank you Dr. Wilson…" I say weakly and she wishes me good luck, reminds me of the pre-natal vitamins, and hangs up.

I stand mechanically and grab my keys. There's a pharmacy store just on the corner, I can find pre-natal vitamins there. I don't register anything until I'm in the vitamin and supplement aisle at the pharmacy and staring at the selection of pre-natal pills. Which brand should I get anyway? There's so much selection, which one is the best? I just grab one at random and pay for it up front. The girl at the register smiles at me almost apologetically.

What does she have to be sorry about? What does she know? I grab the bag and head back home, numb with shock. What the hell do I do now?

Chapter Four

Four Weeks Later

Ali had missed her final. I learned later that she was able to make it up with the head of the history department and she aced it, getting herself an A in the class…but she missed the final. Three days later and I still can't stop thinking about it. Hell, I haven't been able to think about much else since I saw her for the last time as she left the department after making up the final. She looked haunted, tired and…scared, frankly.

The only way Ali could have been able to make up the final was for medical reasons or the passing of an immediate family member. I hope no one in her family died…I hope she's okay. Not that I'd know since I cut off our relationship before it could actually begin. A sudden resolve takes place in my chest. The semester is over and I'm no longer her teacher…I should reach out to her, I should find out what happened, if she's okay.

I stop my pacing and glance outside my bedroom window at the falling snow. Christmas is just a few weeks away and tomorrow everything on campus will be closing for official winter break. I'll have to hurry to campus if I want to try and get a hold of Ali's contact information. I'd only have access to her email if I chose to check my roster online.

Feeling incredibly antsy, I check my watch. It's four thirty, I have time to get to campus, and if I speed, I'll be able to catch my good friend Lucy at the Registrar's office. Lucy has been my buddy since grad school, she appreciates women more than some men do and she always jokes that I'm the best wingman. I give her a call as I make my way through the house.

"Lu, how is my favorite girl doing today?" I ask as soon as she picks up.

"Dr. G! You know me, I'm always well, what can I do for you? I'm kind of busy with end of semester madness," Lu answers good-naturedly and I sigh, I am going to owe her if she agrees to do this for me.

"I need info, Lu." There's a long pause and I close my eyes, hoping she'll help me out. I reach my car and turn on the heat once the car is started. I quickly get any ice off of the windshields and windows before getting in and buckling up.

"On a student, I presume?" She finally asks and I nod as if she can see me.

"Yeah…I just need a phone number for an Alicia King."

Lu sighs deeply and there's another pause. "You know this isn't how things go…but I'll try to get something for you, meet me outside in ten minutes." I thank Lu profusely.

"Yeah, yeah, here's hoping I don't get caught. If I'm successful, you so owe me."

"Whenever you need a wingman Lu I'm your guy. I'll shovel your snow for a week, salt your driveway, whatever you need."

"Alright, alright, don't go hero worshiping on me. I can't be on the phone when I'm in the student records room so I gotta go." I hang up with Lu and practically sped to campus to get there in ten minutes. She walks out of the administration building just as I'm pulling up. I can see a folded piece of paper in her gloved hand. I unlock the car doors and Lu gets into the passenger seat.

"So what do you need this for G? I have to ask." She hands me the paper and I unfold it, practically memorizing the ten digits of Alicia's cell phone number.

"I uh…she was troubled and I really want to make sure she's okay, you know?" I look at Lu and she nods thoughtfully.

"Alright, I get that. Well, you do owe me. I'll be thinking of something epic because I almost got caught in there by the Student Accounts people."

I kiss Lu on the cheek and she bats me away. "Thank you so much, Lu. Like I said, I'm shoveling your snow for a week." I tell her honestly and she rolls her eyes.

"Good, don't be late, come around every morning." I promise her I will and she gets out of the car before jogging back inside and out of the cold. I stare at the piece of paper a second more and pick up my cell phone to dial Ali's number. It rings several times before she answers.

The sound of her voice has me freezing up; I don't know what to say to her. "Hello, who's this?" She says politely, she's always so sweet. My chest constricts and I force myself to speak.

"Hi Ali...it's uh-it's..." I stumble over my words. What the heck is my problem, since when can't I talk to a girl?

"Adam-Dr. G?" She sounds shocked and she corrects herself when she says my name. I hate that she feels she still needs to do that.

"Please call me Adam, never call me Dr. G again." There's a thick silence and I hurry to fill it. "I wanted to make sure that everything is alright with you...you know, with you missing the class final and all." Ali is still silent and I wonder if we've been disconnected. "Are you there, Ali?" I ask before checking the screen on my phone. The call is still connected.

"Yes I'm here...Adam. I need to speak with you, face to face." I jump at the chance to see her again, not even realizing how strange her voice sounds and forgetting the tension coming from her end of the line.

"Of course, do you want to meet up today?" I ask expectantly and practically hold my breath while I wait for her to answer.

"Yes, I think that would be best. Can you meet me…can you meet me at the Boston Coffee House just outside of campus? I'm actually here now." I pull out of the parking space and head to the Coffee House.

"I'll be there in two minutes, I'm leaving from campus." I tell her. She hangs up with a "quiet see you soon" and I focus on the speed limit. The urgency I have to see her and make sure everything is all right with her is overwhelming; she's all that my mind is focused on. I pull into the café's parking lot and nearly forget to lock my car. I need to take a few deep breaths and get it together.

I open the door and step inside, spotting her instantly; she's sitting at a table for two near the window. Her head is down and she's staring intently at her tablet resting on the table. Ali's wearing an oversized lilac sweater and jeans with a pair of light grey snow boots. Her hair is loose, the tight curls falling freely to her back. I think it's gotten longer. She picks up her tea mug and takes a sip before setting it down again.

I finally walk over to her and touch her shoulder. Ali looks up in surprise. "That was fast." She says, mildly impressed. Her eyes seem sad; she still looks tired and worn.

"What's wrong Ali?" I ask and sit down across from her.

She simply stares at me for a moment and then turns slightly to fish something out of her coat that is draped over the back of her chair. It's a small photo shaped rectangle folded in half. She simply hands it to me without a word and I take it slowly. I open it and my brows furrow in confusion.

"What am I looking at?" I ask her and she points to a little black area in the midst of what looks like static, inside the dark oval is a little white circle.

"That's...that's our baby." Oh a baby.
Our...baby...our baby?

"They were able to take a picture of him today...I'm pregnant obviously.... I saw his heartbeat and everything today, too. They say he's healthy so far..." Ali stops talking, her voice shaky and more than nervous.

"Our baby?" I ask her on a broken whisper. She looks me in the eye and nods once. I know then for sure that Ali isn't the type to sleep around. I got her pregnant. I was so worried about ruining her future...and I already did before I even stopped to think of the repercussions if we were having unprotected sex.

"I'm-...Ali I'm so fucking sorry." Emotion I can't describe floods my chest. I'm devastated that I made her life this much harder, she's so young...I hate that I so selfishly had sex with her and then cut her off as if she meant nothing.

Sitting here, seeing the amount of stress she's under, I'm worried about her future...and the baby's. My world abruptly expands and focuses all at once to include Ali and the baby and to focus on them as my top priorities. This moment is more humbling than I could have ever prepared for.

"What are you thinking?" She whispers and I look down at the picture of the ultrasound, at the small bean that's growing inside Ali right now.

"I want to take care of you. You and the baby." Ali's eyes fill with water and I wonder what I said to upset her. Shit, she's pregnant of course she's going to be sensitive. "What's wrong? I didn't mean to upset you. I just...I want to be here for you all the time, I want the baby to never have to worry about anything." Ali sniffles and wipes her eyes.

"I know, I know. I --just-everything has been really difficult since I found out and my parents...they cut me off when they learned about the pregnancy and it's just been hard when faced with doing this alone. I never thought you'd call me or want anything to do with me." I feel a surge of unexpected anger at her parents for abandoning her at such a hard time.

"Is that why you missed the final? You found out you were pregnant?"

Ali shakes her head and she bites her lip nervously. "I had a bout of really bad morning sickness and had an episode from dehydration. A friend of mine drove me to the hospital instead of school." There was so much loaded in her response. The fact that she had to go through that alone infuriates me.

"You could have told me sooner Ali, you should have never assumed that I wanted nothing to do with you, that's just not true." Ali tilts her head at me, giving me a look that is slightly unbelieving. "I mean when faced with something so important, you should have come to me. I'm the father for Pete's sake… What's your situation like?" I ask and her gaze becomes confused at my abrupt change in topic. "You said that your parents cut you off."

Ali's eyes sadden and she nods. "Yeah, they've practically disowned me. I'm lucky to even be on my mother's medical insurance at this point." She sighs and sits back in her chair. "My dad has stopped paying for my apartment, I don't have a job yet, and currently I'm staying with my best friend, Kelsey."

"I want you to move in with me, I have a house on Summit Road, there's more than enough room for you." Ali blinks at me in shock, not expecting me to demand she move in with me, and honestly, I didn't expect it either. But I don't want another instance of where she needs me and I'm not there to take care of her, to help her.

"I can't just…move in with you, Adam. We barely know each other and…problems could arise. I just don't know about that." She says, her voice heavy with hesitation.

"Ali…I have to be there for you. I can't go to bed at night while you're homeless and staying at a friend's house. You can live with me, I have three empty bedrooms and you can move your stuff into one and in a few months, we can move stuff for the baby into another."

Ali chews on her lip, obviously battling with herself. She doesn't want to make a wrong decision. "We'd be like…roommates?" She asks tentatively and I nod, whatever she has to tell herself as long as she's coming home with me.

"I'll even let you pay for groceries when you can manage it, if you want."

Ali releases a deep breath and nods slowly. "Fine, okay. I'll --I'll move in with you." She says in reluctant defeat. "I just don't want to jump into something we could regret down the road…" She looks at me pointedly and I know she's referring to how this all began. How I cut things off and blamed it on school policy.

"That won't happen Ali, you have my word. I'm taking care of you and our baby now. We'll be a family, I promise." I take her hand and hold it in both of mine. "My dad was never around growing up and I don't want that for our Little Bean." I smile at her and for the first time, her expression lightens a bit.

"Little Bean?"

I shrug and glance at the ultra sound. "Doesn't the name suit him so far?" Ali giggles and she nods. It's good to finally see her smile, and hear her laugh. I vow to myself to get her smiling more.

"I guess so, but we aren't naming him that when he comes out," she says firmly, with humor lightening her tone.

"Yeah, he'd be made fun of in school with a name like that." Ali laughs again and I relax a little, pleased with myself. "So all of your things are at your friend's place?" I ask her and she shakes her head, her expression sobering.

"I have to sell some of my furniture and things from my apartment, I have nowhere to put them so most of my stuff is in storage."

I shake my head. "You don't have to do that, you can move everything into my place. I don't have any furniture in my family room and it's pitiful really, what I've got in the kitchen. Plus you can move your bedroom stuff into one of the guest rooms." I smile at her, already things are working out. Thank goodness I have no stylistic eye and have put off decorating the house for so long.

"Are you sure? I can just move my entire apartment into your house?" I nod eagerly and she glances down at her tablet and checks something.

A relieved smile brightens her features once again. "What is it? What's the good news?" I ask and she looks up at me with excitement.

"I got an internship, at a publishing company. It's like an hour's drive away, near the coast, but it's at a publishing company!" I can tell this is the first good news she's heard in weeks. "It's a paid internship too, oh this is so exciting!" Almost instantly her features are suffused with a warm glow, she's almost too beautiful to look at. Our Little Bean would be one cute baby if he looks anything like Ali.

"That's great news, see things are looking up already." I smile at her reassuringly and she smiles thoughtfully.

"Yeah…I guess so."

I pick up the ultrasound and fold it in half to stick into my pocket. "I can keep this, right?"

I ask and she nods, her smile tentative this time. "I have two others in my coat."

"So do you want to see your new home before we start moving your things in?"

"Yeah, I guess we're doing this then." She takes a deep breath and I see her mentally put her big girl pants on. We are doing this, and we're doing it together. I guess I should get my big boy pants on and take a deep breath, too.

Chapter Five

Adam has a really nice house. It's cozy and spacious at the same time. The outside is so unassuming, your standard Connecticut home, snuggled into tall trees which hide the actual size of it. Walking into the foyer, the house smells of pine and cinnamon. A really nice combination, it reminds me of Christmas, which happens to be in less than a few weeks.

Adam takes me through the house, showing me the office, living room, dining room, family room and kitchen. Then upstairs is another family area and four bedrooms with two bathrooms upstairs and one downstairs.

"And there's an apartment above the garage, but I haven't finished putting up the walls in there yet." Adam mentions as we move into the only room with much furniture, the living room. "I've saved up for a long time to buy a house I can fix up on my own. I just didn't realize how exhausting it would be to decorate it too. I guess the place just needs a woman's touch now." Adam smiles at me with a twinkle in his eye and I smirk. I hadn't expected him to be the home renovator type.

"Well, you're lucky my living room furniture pretty much matches the lighter colors of what's in here, we can put it in the family room. My dining room table is small though, it's more of an eat-in kitchen size."

Adam smiles widely. "That's perfect. See how well

things are working for us already?" I almost snort.

"You say that now. I still have to figure out how I'm going to tell Kelsey I'm moving in with you. She kind of hates you. She's assumed you're a playboy who doesn't care about the repercussions of your amorous actions."

Adam surprises me, for the thousandth time today, by laughing instead of getting annoyed or offended. "I understand why she'd think that. How about I go with you to break the news, and then we'll go and get a rental truck to move your stuff out of storage," Adam suggests openly.

I still don't know if it's such a good idea to be moving in with him, but I really have no other options. It's not like I can impose on Kelsey like this when the baby is born. My parents have washed their hands of me, convinced that I've ruined my life, they don't want to support me and an "illegitimate child."

"Hey, where did you go?" Adam snaps me out of my introspection and I give him an apologetic smile.

"Sorry…um, yeah I think it'll be a good idea for us to tell Kelsey together." I nod and Adam stands up, ready to go right away. "She's at work right now so we won't get to her until around three."

"Alright so we'll move you in first then." I want to tell Adam to slow his roll a little bit. Everything is moving so quickly all of a sudden, that I can't wrap my head around any of it.

"Are you tired? We don't have to do it now…or I can take care of it while you rest, if you want."

Adam is studying my expression and I find that I am tired. I have been, ever since I got that call from Dr. Wilson. Sleep hasn't been my friend, but stress has been close to my side.

"Yeah, those circles around your eyes just got darker. Come on, you can sleep in my bed and I'll take care of at least moving your bed into one of the guest rooms. Which one was your favorite?" Adam asks me while he leads me up the stairs holding my hand as if I might drop from exhaustion at any second.

"The one on the right, it had a great view of the trees."

Adam takes me into his room and sits me on his bed. He crouches to remove my boots and socks for me. My heart melts a little at how determined he is to take care of me. This isn't the detached professor who broke things off so coolly in his office; this is the Adam I got a glimpse of the night before. The one who likes old sitcoms and Finding Nemo.

Adam asks me for all the storage information and he tells me he'll be back in an hour, or two, at the most. I nod, my head falling down on one of his pillows as if by magnetic attraction. Adam smiles at me and tells me to rest before he disappears through the bedroom door.

***

I wake to the sound of Kelsey's ring tone blaring into my skull. I fish my cell phone from under the pillow. When did it get there?

"Hello?" I answer groggily and Kelsey yells at me from the other line.

Her voice alarmed and accusing. "What the hell Ali, you're moving in with him?"

Oh crap, I check the time quickly, it's almost nine at night. I slept all day.

"Calm down Kels, I was going to talk to you about it but I fell asleep. Where are you?" I ask her and she sighs in frustration.

"I'm at my apartment, I just got a call from professor baby daddy that you wouldn't be here tonight because you fell asleep at his place and, I quote, "we have to talk to you about something tomorrow." I'm not stupid; I put two and two together. I thought you weren't in contact with Adam at all." I sigh and sit up while brushing my hair out of my face.

"He called me today…I don't know how he got my number, but he called and we met up after my appointment and I told him. He's really adamant, he wants to take care of the baby and me. What better option do I have? I can't impose on you forever, Kelsey. You snore really loud." Kelsey laughs reluctantly and I relax, that's Kels for you, never one for a grudge.

"Whatever, bitch, my snoring is ambient and you know it. It helps with REM."

We both crack up and I sigh. "A lot is changing…I got that internship, by the way, at Ranch House."Kelsey squeals in excitement, her mood already having done a one-eighty, and she congratulates me. "See! Things are looking up, you'll start working there and they'll realize how much of a genius you are and make you an editor right away." I giggle at Kelsey's optimism.

"One can only hope. Anyway are you cool with this? Me moving in with Adam?" I ask and hold my breath.

"Yeah girl, I understand. I'm actually glad he stepped up to take care of you and the Little Bun. Someone has to."

I laugh, and tell Kelsey the baby's new name. "Little Bean? Yeah we're definitely not letting him name the baby."

"But your name for him isn't that different." I snort and I can almost hear Kelsey rolling her eyes.

"Bun is completely different from Bean. Plus it's unisex, just because you keep calling it 'he' doesn't mean it's gonna be a boy."

I laugh at her odd reasoning and shake my head fondly. "Well we don't have to think about definite names until we know the sex of the baby for sure. I can't help but think it's going to be a boy, though." I say a bit dreamily. It would be perfect to have a little mixed baby boy with curly brown hair and his father's blue eyes.

"Well I've already picked up the big book of baby names so you better call me over when you guys start to think about what to call him for sure." I promise Kelsey that she'll be as involved with everything as she wants to be.

I like the fact that my baby will at least have a God Mother who loves him. Kelsey and I stay on the line for another twenty minutes fantasizing about the future. It's easy to sit back and imagine a life full of happy memories with her, Adam, the baby and I. When I finally end the call, I can't deny the wave of sadness that envelops me when I am reminded that Little Bean won't know his grandparents and might not know his uncles either.

"You're awake. I thought you were going to be asleep for the rest of the day." Adam walks into his room and lounges on the bed next to me, his hand propping his head up as his eyes scan my face.

"Kelsey woke me up, I just got off of the phone with her." Adam looks guilty and he starts to apologize but I shake my head dismissively. "It's fine, really. Kelsey isn't one to get upset and hold a grudge. She understands and we're good." Adam nods and he sits up, folding his legs in and running a hand through his hair. I realize belatedly that he is shirtless…wearing only pajama bottoms.

"She was pissed with me when I called her. I'd be pissed with me too, I guess." I force my eyes from his chest and stomach up to his intense gaze.

"She doesn't hate you, it's alright." Adam licks his lips distractingly and his features fall into further upset.

"I bet your family does, though." At the mention of them my jaw locks and I force myself not to get worked up.

"They want nothing to do with me, so be it. We don't have to waste a thought and energy over their feelings." I snap at him unintentionally and Adam purses his lips, but doesn't continue with that subject.

"There is food downstairs, I made steak fajitas." Adam gets up from the queen sized bed and pulls me up. I am really hungry, I didn't eat much today.

Once in the kitchen Adam fixes me a couple of fajitas over a bed of salad. This looks like something I'd order out of a restaurant.

"You cook too?" I ask him, impressed.

He smiles cockily, flashing his teeth and winking at me. "I do it all, baby." I giggle and take a bite of the fajita. It's delicious.

"My goodness this tastes like…" I grasp for an appropriate synonym and the only word that pops into my head is 'sex'.

"Oh don't worry, I know, I know." He says jokingly and winks. He watches me eat and I break the silence.

"Did you eat already?" I ask and he nods before resting against the island bar.

"I managed to get all your stuff moved in too, I hope you don't mind, I had my cousin help me. He owns a moving company not too far from campus." My eyebrows raise, I never thought to ask Adam about his family.

"Do you have any brothers or sisters?"

Adam shakes his head. "No, I was raised by my mom and my aunt. My cousin and I grew up like brothers. They are my only family. I gotta tell you my mom will be thrilled she's finally getting a grandbaby. There's nothing worse than a Polish woman moaning about how she'll die before she gets to see her grandchildren in real life." I laugh, clearly envisioning a loving mother doting on her son to settle down and have a family.

"I'm sure she envisioned you to be married first, though…" I say and Adam's expression sobers.

"No, she'll pretty much be happy, either way. As long as the baby will have a loving mother and father she'll be happy." I hear the double meaning to his words loud and clear. He wants me to be happy with the fact that Little Bean will have Adam and I in his life, we don't need my parents.

"So I was thinking that tomorrow we could go shopping for a Christmas tree after we get the rest of your stuff from Kelsey's place." Adam changes the subject and I'm glad for it.

"Yeah of course, I love Christmas time, putting up the tree especially." Adam smiles, satisfied.

"Me too...my mother and aunt and cousin will be over for that tomorrow, so you'll get to meet them." Adam adds that as a casual aside and my eyes widen. I can't remember the last time I've had to make a good impression on someone's parents. Now I'm meeting Adam's entire family in one night?

"Um...okay." I reply, at a loss, and Adam smiles at me apologetically.

"I know this is all fast, but you'll like them, and they'll love you, I promise." I hope he's right.

"But won't it come as a shock to them...? That you got one of your students pregnant and she's now living with you and everything?" I ask, my words nearly stumbling over each other.

"I told them already..." Adam informs me and I relax a little more.

"Well, okay then." Wide eyed, I take another bite of fajita.

"So when do you start your internship?"

I tell Adam about the position as an Editor's assistant

and that I'd start the Monday after New Year's Day. They'll be paying me half of what a regular Editor's assistant would be making, of course, since I'm an intern. But since I'm graduating soon, it can very easily turn into a full-blown position at the company. They're a smaller publishing house but growing, and it's a great opportunity for the future. I'd be doing exactly what I've dreamed about doing for so long now.

After I finish eating, Adam shows me the eat-in kitchen area and I recognize my dining room set. The round glass table with wooden base and complementing dining chairs go surprisingly well with the space and color scheme of the kitchen. We move into the family room and I see my furniture doesn't look half bad in the space, though its apartment sized so it's not half bad. Moving on upstairs into my room everything looks exactly as I had it set up in my apartment.

My chest tightens when I realize he must have remembered exactly how it was set up from when he spent the night at my place. I hug Adam tightly when I thank him and kiss him on the cheek goodnight before he walks down the hall to his room. I take a deep breath and release almost all of the stress that has been my companion for the last few weeks. If Adam was going to step up and be a father to Little Bean then we'd be okay.

Chapter Six

My mom walks into the house and kisses me on both cheeks before demanding to know where Ali is, in fluent Polish. My mother, Halina, is sixty-five, yet looks not a day over forty. How our family inherited such good genes, I will never know; usually we Polish age like cheese rather than wine. Following my mom in, is her sister, my aunt Ania. She kisses me on the cheek and hurries in from the cold. My cousin Gabriel is last through the door, he touches his knuckles to mine and I shut the door behind them.

"So where is she? We're all eager to meet her, Adi." My mother asks me in English this time, using her nickname for me, I gesture for them to walk into the family room. My mother is at the head of the pack to go and meet Ali.

Ali is just stepping out of the kitchen with a bottle of water in hand and she sets it down when she sees us all enter the wide-open space. She smiles shyly, but genuinely and something shifts into place in my chest. I can't explain it, but this feels right.

"Look at how beautiful my new daughter is!" My mother instantly falls in love with Ali, which is understandable, and pulls her into a warm hug. Mom holds Ali at arm's length and aunt Ania studies Ali along with her sister and finally smiles warmly. Ania steals Ali from my mom and embraces her in a tight hug.

"Ali, this is my mother, mama Lina, and my aunt

Ania. Oh and this is my cousin Gabriel." I tack on and Ali laughs at the look on Gabriel's face at my almost forgetting about him.

"Yeah I only grew up with the man and he forgets about me. Classic." Gabriel says jokingly and surprises I think, everyone in the room, apart from Ali, by hugging her in greeting. Gabriel isn't one for affection; he only ever hugs or kisses his mom and his wife, who had to work late tonight and couldn't be here. So this is new, to say the least.

"It's nice to meet you all, sorry if I'm a little shy." Ali says, sweet as ever. I want to tuck her into my side to make her feel more comfortable. Mama Lina obviously has the same thought and takes Ali's hand, attaching herself to Ali's side.

"No need for this shyness Ali, you are family." I've never been so grateful for my mom as I am now. I swear that woman is the best I know.

The night goes amazingly well. Ali really hits it off with my mom and aunt, subsequently gaining approval from Gabriel. To see Ali having such a good time decorating the tree and joking around with my family makes me unexplainably possessive. Ali's place is here with me and I want her to feel the same way I do.

An idea forms in my head and takes root when my family gets ready to leave. Ali promises to stop by my mother and aunt's house to learn how Christmas Eve Uszka is made. I want Ali to have all of her family around her, especially during holiday season. She has to be feeling lonely, not being able to talk to her own mom and carry on their Christmas traditions. When I used Ali's phone to get Kelsey's phone number earlier, I snagged her parents' numbers too. It says a lot that Ali has them under their formal names and not 'mom' or 'dad'.

"I really like your family. Your mom especially, she's great." Ali says after they've all left. She washes the last bit of dishes and starts to dry them.

"Yeah, I could tell they really love you, I told you they would." I smile knowingly and Ali bumps me with her hip playfully, smiling to herself.

Her hair is pulled up into a ponytail and the usual curly culprits fall into her face. My fingers itch to brush them behind her ear, but I just don't know how she'll take that. Or if she even wants me to touch her intimately ever again.

I watch her move around the kitchen for a moment and decide that I'll never know for sure if I don't try. Stepping forward to intercept her on the way back to the dish drying rack, I go all in and cup her face in my hands to press a soft kiss to her lips. Ali gasps, shock stilling her completely.

My hands move from her face to pull her waist closer to mine. After a moment's hesitation, she softens and melts into me willingly. Her plush lips move against mine in a heated kiss. My hands are just about to slide down to cup her round bottom when she breaks the kiss and pulls away.

"I didn't…expect that." She whispers almost hoarsely as she tries to calm her breathing. I see the heat in her eyes before she can control it.

"Didn't expect that I'd still want you like this?" I ask, trying to get into her head.

Her eyes are unsure and I watch for any other emotion to cross her features "No…yes…I didn't expect you to kiss me. This would make things complicated, we're supposed to be more like roommates, remember?"

I shake my head and decide to be straight up with her. "Ali I let you think that so you'd feel comfortable moving in with me…I want you, I still want you. That hasn't changed even though I tried to force it to, it hasn't changed."

Ali stares at me wide eyed and I watch as a question takes form in her mind. "You want me…but you still don't know why you do, correct?"

I take a deep breath and then sigh as I exhale. "You're special…I don't know why yet, you're right about that, but you're special to me and I won't deny it anymore."

Ali's eyes scan my face and she bites that delicious lip, her expression still unsure. "I don't know how I feel about this yet Adam, everything is just happening so fast, can you just let me catch up a bit?"

I nod. If she needs time I can give it. As long as she comes here every day and calls my house home, I can give her time. After all, she is pregnant with my baby.

"That's perfectly fine. As long as you know where I stand." Ali nods and she silently continues on with the dishes.

I decide to leave her to her thoughts, hoping they are about how much I just turned her on. I head out back to make a couple of phone calls. The only way I'll prove to Ali that I'm not just messing around and I really want something with her, is if I fix her relationship with her parents. I'll do just that. After pulling on my coat and grabbing my gloves, I walk into the softly falling snow. Nothing is sticking to the ground yet, but give it a couple of days and that will definitely change.

I pull out my phone and dial 'Shatrice King (Ali's mom).' She answers on the third ring.

"Hello, how can I help you?" She has the efficient tone of someone who maybe works in a hospital setting, getting right down to business with no time to waste. I can hear an echo of Ali's voice in her mother's.

"Hi this is Adam-Adam Gwozdek. We've never had the chance to formally meet or anything, but I'm…" I pause, unsure of how to continue that sentence, what was I to Ali? Her teacher? The man that got her pregnant? Her baby daddy?

"You're the man who got my daughter pregnant and ruined her life." Mrs. King finishes for me crisply and I press my lips together. This is going to be harder than I thought. I figured Ali's mother would be easier to appeal to.

"I got her pregnant, yes, but I did not ruin her life. You did that—excuse me you and your husband did that by cutting her off and practically throwing her out on the street to fend for herself." I close my eyes in horror at what I just said and how sharply I said it. This isn't going to go well.

"I wouldn't expect you to understand right now, Adam, but the moment your child makes a stupid mistake that will color the rest of her life for the worst, you can get back to me. How could you expect us to possibly support Alicia and an illegitimate child?

God forbid, she feels she could take advantage of us and get pregnant again after the kid is born! She would only be on a downhill spiral and we simply cut her off so she won't do any damage to my husband and I and the rest of our family." Disgusted, I begin to see why Ali won't even talk about them.

"Do you have any idea of how shallow you sound? You make it as if Ali is sixteen and a teen mom. She'll be graduating from college by the time the baby is born and is already starting her career. How you could abandon your own child in such a time of need is despicable." I'm beyond livid and I don't care for choosing my words carefully anymore.

"Ha! A career is not in reading books. We thought we could eventually sway her to a better path there, but it became too much when she got pregnant, that we can't change." The woman's tone is so final it sounds as if Ali is dead to her. "I thought I raised Ali right, not to be the kind of girl that gets pregnant out of wedlock.

It's the worse disappointment to realize that I failed as a parent." Shatrice says this as if it were a thought running through her mind. "I'm sorry, Adam but there is nothing you can say or do. We want nothing to do with Alicia." With that, the line goes dead.

Frustrated beyond belief, I chuck my phone into the woods behind the house and groan in angered exasperation. After several deep breaths I go find my phone and slip it into my pants pocket before heading back into the house. Ali is curled up on the couch watching TV and sipping a cup of tea.

"What were you doing out there? It's too cold to be outside."

I hang up my coat and slide the glass door closed before stepping fully into the family room.

"I had to take a phone call. What are you watching?" I sit on the couch next to Ali and drape an arm around her shoulders, stealing some of her warmth. She stiffens for a fraction of a second before relaxing against me.

"The Polar Express. It's one of my favorite Christmas

movies." I smile, Ali will make a good mom. I think the only mom who would actually enjoy sitting through cartoons and kid movies with Little Bean.

"Do you know all the words to this one too?" I tease and she smiles at me slyly before proceeding to recite every line in tandem with the characters. I can't help but laugh and she giggles. The sound does more to warm me than the crackling fire across from us. This would never get old, that's for sure.

Ali falls asleep against my chest while watching the other Christmas specials. She feels so good against me that I don't dare wake her or take her upstairs to her room. Instead, I stretch out along the couch and fall asleep beside her.

In the morning, my phone vibrating in my pants pocket wakes us both. Ali stirs and I fish the phone out of my pocket awkwardly while holding her against me securely. It's just my fucking luck that the phone falls face up onto the floor and the name Shawn King is displayed bright and bold for Ali's waking eyes to see.

"What…why is my dad calling you?" She sits up and grabs my phone from the floor. I'm at a loss for words as she looks at me for an explanation, one I haven't quite formulated yet. She hands the phone to me and crosses her arms over her chest. "Well, answer it," she says angrily and I send her a pleading glance before answering the phone.

"Hello?" Ali watches me closely and my heart

hammers in my chest. This is so not the time to screw up with her.

"Adam Gwozdek, correct?" The man's deep, authoritative voice sounds across the line and I give him the confirmation. "I decided to give you a call before you tried my cell. I understand you think you mean well in this mess, but do not call my wife again. You have no right to harass us over a decision we made concerning our daughter." My jaw clenches in anger at the brisk tone of his voice.

"Fine, I understand, sir," I say with reluctance.

There's no arguing with him in front of Ali. Without a reply, he hangs up the phone. Ali gives me a look; she doesn't even have to explain why it's a bad idea to reach out to her parents. I know now. She simply stands and walks upstairs, shaking her head.

Chapter 7

She's pissed at me. It's obvious, as she hasn't said a word in my direction all morning, not even when I left and came back from shoveling snow at Lucy's. Just when I might have been making a little headway, I have to go and screw this up. Frustrated with myself, I pace around my bedroom trying to come up with my next move.

I know Ali has two older brothers...I wonder what her relationships with them is like. I could give one of them a call and try and get some help to make Ali's parents see reason. But then, that would require me to steal Ali's phone again for their numbers and I'm pretty sure she'll move out at that point. Exasperated with myself, I sigh and flop down on the bed.

My phone rings and I see it's Ali's friend Kelsey calling me. Why would Kelsey be calling me? I stand up and walk over to my window, glancing out at the driveway, I see Ali's car is still parked there.

I answer the phone, not knowing what to expect. "Hey, uh...Adam?" Kelsey greets me, unsure of whether I'm Adam or Dr. G. I stifle my sigh.

"Hi Kelsey, is everything alright?" I ask, more than curious as to what this call will be about.

"Yeah everything is fine, how are you doing?" I pause, at a loss. Why is she making small talk?

"I'm fine Kelsey…what's up?" I ask, growing a little impatient.

"So I heard you've somehow gotten in touch with Ali's parents…" Kelsey is talking as if we're spies who may or may not be on the same team.

"Have you just spoken to Ali? Is she mad at me?" I ask quickly and Kelsey urges me to calm down.

"She's not mad, a little annoyed, but really she's just trying to deal with the hurt of her mom and dad turning their backs on her. She's been trying to ignore it, but honestly I'm glad she's dealing with it now. Repressed stress and heartache can't be good for the baby. Especially in the first trimester." I start to pace again, feeling anxious for Ali. I should just knock on her door and let her yell at me, then hold her so she knows she's not alone.

"Can we get to the point a little quicker, Kelsey, please?" I try to temper my tone so that I don't sound as worked up as I feel.

"I'd like to help you. Whether you want to kick her parent's asses or what, I'll help you fix their relationship." A sliver of hope needles its way into my chest and I smile.

"You're an angel Kelsey, an absolute angel." Kelsey laughs and says something about how everyone else knows this. I don't really pay attention, instead I wonder if Kelsey might have a way to contact Ali's brothers. "Kelsey do you have the number to either brother's cell phones? Ali's brothers." I clarify and smile when she says she has both. I quickly jot down both Tristan and Trenton's phone numbers.

"So are you going to call them? What will you say? You need to have a game plan you know, so nothing blows up in your face like before." Kelsey is right. I do need a game plan.

"What do you suggest?" Kelsey pauses for a moment and I roll my eyes. Must she drag this out?

"Well, Ali and her brothers get along well enough, but she secretly resents them because they are clearly the favorites. On Tristan and Trenton's end, they adore their little sister, they are just a bit oblivious when it comes to Ali and her relationship with Shatrice and Shawn. So call Trenton, because his job isn't as demanding as Tristan's and he's actually flying in tomorrow. Trent and Tristan don't yet know about what happened, they don't even know that Ali is pregnant."

"How do you think Trenton will react when the guy that got his little sister pregnant calls to tell him the 'good news'?" If I had a little sister who I loved on any level and her professor called me to tell me that she's pregnant with his baby, and subsequently disowned by her parents, I'd fly in early just to kick his ass.

"Well I never said this would be easy, Adam, but we have to try something. Ali and the baby can't live a life without an entire half of their family who's out there breathing the same air." Kelsey is right, and what the hell am I doing doubting myself? I have to try everything before I give in to doubt.

"Thank you, Kelsey, I'll call you later with an update…actually why don't you come over and keep Ali company?" I offer, knowing Ali might ignore me for the rest of the day.

"Actually, she invited me over already and I'm leaving my apartment now, I just wanted to have this conversation before I got there, so she wouldn't overhear us." I'm beginning to see why this Kelsey girl is Ali's closest friend.

"Alright Kelsey, I'll see you soon then." I let her go and pull on some boots and a belt. I'll go pick up some take-out for the girls so it gives me an excuse to make this call. I take a deep breath; I hope this works for Ali's sake.

I'm just about to step out of the bedroom when Ali knocks on the door before gently pushing it open to peek inside. "Hi." She says softly and I pull her inside, she surprises me by giving me a tight hug. I wrap my arms around her and inhale. She smells like caramel, the scent is quickly becoming my favorite. "I know you mean well, Adam, but please don't waste your time on my parents. I've come to terms with it and…it's okay if they're not in our lives."

A very vivid image takes form in my head of me one day marrying Ali, who will walk her down the aisle? I blink away the thought, confused by it. More confused by the wealth of yearning attached to it. I want Ali to be my wife, dammit; I want us to be a family. "I can't help it Ali, I just...I want to make things right for you." My voice is full of emotion and she pulls away slightly, her gaze locking onto mine, searching.

"Adam really, it's okay." She says finally and I sigh, nodding.

Fine, I'll let her think I was giving up, but I'm still making that call. Ali pulls away and glances out of the window while pushing a strand of hair behind her ear.

"My friend Kelsey is coming over, I hope that's okay?" I nod and smile teasingly at her.

"This is your place too, remember...roomie." I wink at her and she laughs.

"Right..." As if on cue, Kelsey pulls into the driveway and hurries out of the car and up onto the porch. Ali and I head downstairs and she lets Kelsey in. Kelsey is an attractive girl, I noticed it the first time I met her when Ali and I went by her apartment to pack up Ali's things. Seeing them together again reminds me how much Ali has her beat. Kelsey knows it, I know it...Ali is the only oblivious one and that's what makes her so noticeable.

"Hey Adam, how's it goin'?" After hugging Ali in greeting, Kelsey notices me by the coat closet and puts on the perfect act. As if we didn't just have a covert conversation over the phone less than ten minutes ago.

"Good to see you again, Kelsey. So what are you girls gonna be up to?" I ask while the two walk through to the family room.

"We're just hanging out, might watch a couple of movies, the usual," Ali answers and I follow them, heading into the kitchen for a bottle of water.

"Alright, how about I go pick up some pizza or Chinese or maybe…" I wonder what other take-out places are around here.

"Oh there's this really great Caribbean spot by Ali's…old place, that's really good." Kelsey stumbles a little at the mention of the apartment Ali's parent's kicked her out of.

"Actually I've been craving some Ox Tail with rice and beans." Ali says dreamily, as if she's imagining the food already.

I get the directions to the place from Kelsey and they tell me what they want and recommend something I should try from the restaurant. I've heard of Jerk Chicken but never actually tried it. There's a first time for everything. I head to the car and pull out my phone to dial Trenton. If he's in California, then it's only one thirty there. Once I'm in the car and halfway to the restaurant, I dial Trenton's number.

"Hello, this is Trenton speaking." Trent's voice fills

the car speakers and he sounds so much like his intimidating father I almost take pause.

"Trenton, this is Adam Gwozdek…I have to talk to you about Ali." There's no need to bring up the whole professor detail so soon.

"As in my sister, Alicia?" Trenton's voice loses the professional clip and becomes a little more familiar. If he's anything like his parents, oh how that will change.

"Yes. Can I ask that you listen with an open mind and not hang up on me until I'm through explaining everything?" There's a pause, I hear a door open and close.

"Alright Adam…go ahead." Trenton sighs and I launch ahead with the story, telling him everything truthfully and as I see it.

"You got my baby sister pregnant?" Is the first question he asks, his voice filled with incredulity. By now, I'm simply parked outside of the restaurant's building and wondering how the rest of this conversation will go.

"Yeah…she's close to seven weeks along now."

Trenton curses, his tone still in shocked disbelief. "So she's staying at your place because my parents, who have yet to tell either my brother or me about this, by the way, cut her off and won't have anything to do with her." Trenton verifies, trying to get all the facts together.

"Yeah man, exactly. I mean of course I would've moved her in with me even if she did still have her apartment, but yeah that's correct." I rub my hands against my jeans. He hasn't hung up on me yet, which is good.

"I can't believe this…I just can't believe I was so blind to their relationship. That it was so fickle. I'm going to talk to my brother and we'll figure something out with our parents. Just don't call them again is all I'd advise…and take care of my sister, man."

I promise Trenton that Ali's my top priority and he says he'll give me a call when he's flown in so he can visit Ali. Once the call is ended, I release a deep sigh of relief and finally head into the restaurant to get the food.

I walk into the house with two bags of food and a small grin. I can't help but feel that I'm getting somewhere with Ali's family. Which feels really good. I'm surprised to see my mother and aunt sitting in the family room with Ali and Kelsey. I didn't even see their cars in the driveway.

"Ma, Aunt Ania, what are you two doing here?" I put the food down on the island bar and step into the family room to kiss both women.

"Mama Lina called to ask if she could come over. They were bored at their house." Ali answers before my mother could. I notice her arm firmly around Ali's shoulders and I wonder what bonding went down in here. Kelsey looks dewy eyed, and the same for my aunt.

"Yes and I brought some pictures for you to put in frames around the house. Now that you have done all your additions and renovations it's time to make this place a home." My mom informs me pointedly and I glance around. The place is kind of like a model home, in that there aren't any real personal touches.

"So I guess it's good that I got extra food, I didn't know if I wanted the Jerk Chicken, the fish that looked too good to pass up, or something called Roti that smelled amazing." Both Ali and Kelsey laugh at me.

"You should try all of them and see what you like more." Ali suggests while all the women get up to come fix plates for themselves.

"That's the plan." I wink at her and she smiles, giggling softly. I glance up from the food over at my mom who tastes everything before she settles on the fish. I want to ask her what was up with all the crying that must have been going on while I was gone. "So mama, where are the pictures you said you brought?" I ask casually, she knows me well enough to know I want to talk to her alone.

"Oh, I'll show you where I left them." Lina leads me upstairs to my room. I notice a photo album has been placed on my bed. "Please tell me you are the son I raised and trying your hardest to make sure Alicia's mother will be in her life." Is the first thing my mother asks me once the door is closed.

"Of course, mom." Lina nods and sits down on the bed, taking up the photo album.

"Good, the poor girl looked so sad when Ania and I arrived, just about ready to burst into tears. When I finally pulled the story out of her and her friend, I was simply appalled. The words her mother said to her aren't words a mother should utter to their child. Ever." My eyebrows furrow and I wonder how bad it could be…based on the conversation I had with Shatrice I can't imagine it would be any better, and that's bad enough.

"Adam, you do intend to marry Ali don't you?" I knew that question was coming sooner or later.

I smile at my mom and answer without hesitation. "I do mom, I just have to get her to want me just as much." Lina nods, satisfied with my reply.

"I am always proud of you my son, never forget this." She stands up and takes me into a motherly hug.

"I love you, mama." With a kiss on her cheek we both head back downstairs.

Chapter 8

I stare sightlessly at the calendar on the side of Adam's fridge. Two weeks until Christmas and that's usually when Trist and Trent come home for the holidays. I wonder if they've gotten the Christmas tree already. Usually mom and dad wait until the boys were home from college, internships, or work, to get the Christmas tree and decorate it. It was a tradition that we all pick out the tree together and decorate it together. I guess there wouldn't be any 'together' including me anymore.

"Hey you, what are you doing up so early?" Adam walks into the kitchen, shirtless and sleepy, his hair flopping into his face while he rubs his eyes.

"I thought I'd make you some coffee and get breakfast going." I rid myself of all thoughts surrounding my parents and smile up at Adam who is now standing directly in front of me, studying me closely.

"Sure, but we're going out today. I hope you know how to ice skate." Adam smiles at me lopsidedly and I grin.

"Oh please, I can skate circles around pretty much anyone." I say haughtily and Adam lets out a surprised laugh.

"I think that's a challenge I have to meet."

I grin saucily at him and turn around to get some

coffee going for him. I think I just miss coffee in general. I'll take a nice Cuban Coffee over tea any day.

"So what were you going to make for breakfast?" Adam's voice is surprisingly close to my ear, his breath tickles my neck and I tense. Every time he gets close to me like this, it's dangerous. I don't know if it's my living with him or the pregnancy, but I've been more sensitive lately. Adam is everywhere, even in my dreams and he's wearing on my resolve to distance myself from him a little.

"Um…I was going to make some bacon, eggs and biscuits." Adam presses up behind me and places his hand on my waist. He reaches over me for a coffee mug as an excuse to touch me I'm sure. But he achieves his desired effect on me and I have to hold my breath until he moves away to open the fridge.

"I'll help you." He pulls out the eggs, bacon, and biscuit dough before brushing behind me once more. There's enough space in the kitchen so he doesn't have to do that, but obviously he's trying to achieve something and it's working perfectly…though he doesn't know that. Yet.

"I'm glad you know how to use the oven…I've always been scared of that thing since I was small." Adam admits to me and I can't help but laugh at him. "Seriously, I have a vivid memory of my mother opening the oven while I was right next to it, the heat that came out just shocked me. I thought I was set on fire."

I laugh again, harder this time and Adam smiles at me. "I'm sorry, it's obvious you were badly scarred by this. But it's really funny. So you won't even make frozen pizza?"

Adam shakes his head, his eyes wide. "Nope. I won't get near a hot oven." I giggle and he smiles at me boyishly. "I love the sound of your laugh." I bite my lip, not expecting him to say that. Really he says the sweetest things at the oddest times.

"Well we might have to work on that fear." I tease.

Adam quirks his eyebrow at me, "Good luck with that, my mom has tried ever since I was three and it hasn't worked."

I chuckle while popping the biscuits out of the packaging and laying them on a baking sheet. "Well I'm going to preheat it now so…just a warning." Adam gives the oven a wide birth when I set it to pre-heat. He starts on the eggs and I watch him crack a few into a bowl. The unhindered view of his well-defined chest and arms are extremely distracting.

"You like what you see?" Adam catches me watching and smirks, his eyes roaming from my lips down to my chest, hips, and back. I feel the heat of his gaze like a tangible caress and I shiver.

"Well obviously. Little Bean is an answer to that." I place my hand on my still flat stomach and Adam stops what he's doing.

He walks over to me and gets down on his knees in front of me. The last time he was like this was in his classroom, I was half-naked and blind with need for him. Adam encircles my waist with his arms, pulling me closer to him and he kisses just under my belly button. I shiver again and he glances up at me. His eyes hot on mine.

My breathing hitches and Adam lifts my shirt to press another kiss on the same spot, this time, against my sensitive skin. I sway towards him, my eyes closing at the sensations that take over, spreading through my veins in waves.

"What do you want, Ali?" Adam asks huskily and I open my eyes to look down at him. All I can think about is his mouth on me, sliding down to even more sensitive areas. Adam kisses me again, this time lower and I can't help the shiver that works its way up my spine. "Answer me, Ali." Adam murmurs and I inhale sharply when he nips at my skin with his teeth.

"Adam...I..." I can't get my thoughts together and I swear my vision is tunneling to Adam solely.

"Do you want me to stop?" He asks this time and I shake my head.

I don't have the faculties to think rationally at the moment. Adam picks me up and sits me on the counter. He pulls off my pajama bottoms and panties in one swift motion. I gasp when his mouth goes directly to my already wet folds. I brace myself against the counter and cry out when his tongue flicks out against my clitoris, swiping up and down in swift licks. Adam moans in pleasure, the sound reverberating against me and I can't help but call out his name. Adam slows his pace, as if savoring me. He sucks on my sensitive skin and nibbles on my clit. I arch against his wonderful mouth, wanting more. Adam thrusts his tongue into me over and over and I rub myself against his mouth, my orgasm building impossibly high. Just when I'm about to tip over the edge Adam pulls away and I cry out in shock. How dare he stop when I'm so close? Adam blows on my clitoris and slips his finger into me.

"Adam!" I nearly scream as the orgasm crushes me, an avalanche of heightened sensation and pleasure. Before I can fully come down from my climax Adam is pushing his thick length into me, his pace deliciously slow. Adam pulls my hands from their death grip on the counter to his broad shoulders.

My fingers dig into his skin and he hisses, pushing into me harder and deeper. "Adam," His name is a prayer on my lips. Adam isn't rushed or hurried. He takes his time with me. His lips are seemingly everywhere all at once as he pushes into me and withdraws with agonizing slowness.

"You're so beautiful baby, I've wanted inside this tight piece of heaven ever since I saw you at the coffee house." Adam whispers hoarsely in my ear just as he slams into me, touching so deep that I feel something at my very core quiver, sending waves of indescribable pleasure through me. I gasp Adam's name and he does it again. Adam holds me firmly and pushes deep once more.

"Come for me Ali…let me feel you clench and quiver around me, baby." I cry out at his heated words and he slams into me again, kicking off a mind-blowing release, all I can do is hold onto him and let wave after of wave of pleasure course through me.

When I come back to Earth, I realize we're both on the floor. I'm straddling Adam and he's still very much buried inside me. We are both panting and I'm pretty sure I no longer have command over my muscles. I rest my head on Adam's shoulder and we sit like this until our breathing returns to normal.

"We should definitely do that more often." Adam says and I stifle a giggle.

We really shouldn't have crossed this line. Now things will be complicated. Adam lifts me up so he can slide out of me. He carries me easily to the half bath off the family room and cleans me up.

"Adam what was that…?" I ask him, I'm really hoping for an honest answer.

"Ali, there's no secret that I want you, how could I not?" He answers simply and I almost jump at the sound of the oven beeping, alerting me that it's done pre-heating. "Another reason why I hate ovens." Adam grumbles and I don't hide my laugh this time.

Adam and I manage to finish making breakfast and we sit at the table to eat. Adam keeps glancing at me, almost as if he is unsure of something. I tilt my head at him and raise an eyebrow, wanting to know what he's thinking.

"I know you don't particularly like this subject but…don't you have two brothers?" Adam asks carefully and I nod, wondering why he's all of a sudden bringing them up. "Do you have a good relationship with them?" I shrug; I mean I guess so, when away from my parent's, my brothers and I get along like any other normal siblings.

"Yes, I guess we do, why?" It's Adam's turn to shrug as he pokes at his eggs with the fork absently.

"Just wondering." I take a bite of my biscuit and Adam studies me again. "If you could…would you want to have a relationship with your parents?"

I hold in my sigh. I can't get upset at Adam, I really haven't told him anything about what happened between my parents and I, other than the fact that they washed their hands of me.

"Not unless they apologize to me. My mother in particular said some really hurtful things to me. My father was just shallow and…callous." Adam is still looking at me expectantly, wanting me to go on. "She said that I wouldn't amount to anything…because to her I'm worthless. That I might as well be on the streets with other girls who sleep around and get pregnant."

"My father said that he doesn't want me linked to his

family anymore. That I'd just drag their name through the mud...what with my brother working in the White House and my father being such a successful lawyer." I finish emotionlessly. I'm through crying over their words that stabbed me in the back like the sharpest daggers.

"I...I have no words Ali that's just...that's fucked up." Adam says vehemently and he shakes his head, his eyebrows furrowing.

"It is what it is. I'd really rather not talk about it or them anymore, past this point, Adam." I tell him firmly and he nods, his eyes searching my gaze.

"I get it. I won't bring them up again." I sigh in relief and we finish our breakfast in silence.

After the dishes are washed and put away, Adam follows me upstairs, reminding me to get ready for ice-skating. My mood lightens as I look forward to gliding around on the ice with Adam. I can't help but picture this ridiculously romantic moment where Adam and I turn into pro skaters and complement each other on the ice.

"Ready?" Adam asks me as I step out of my room dressed for the day.

"Yeah." I smile at him shyly and he cups my face in his hand, surprising me, to press his lips to mine. Once, twice, and a third time.

"I love your smile." I have to blink a couple of times

to bring myself back into focus. "When we get back…I think we should talk about you moving into the master bedroom with me." Adam kisses me again and then takes my hand and we head out to go ice skating.

"I know this little pond not too far from here, it's private, not many people know about it." Adam and I walk into the wooded area behind all the houses and we take a walk along a footpath where the snow isn't as deep. Soon, there is a break in the trees and we come across a medium sized pond that looks completely frozen over.

There isn't anyone around but us. I spot a park bench and slip my skates from my shoulder. I had tied the laces together and slung them over my shoulder before we left, Adam doing the same. I go have a seat to put my skates on and glide out onto the ice once I'm ready.

I skate around the circumference of the pond a few times before Adam joins me, smiling as he skates backwards to face me as we go around.

"Show off." I stick my tongue out at him and he laughs.

"I told you, I'm a pro when it comes the ice." I roll my eyes and remember him telling me he does play hockey for fun.

"I bet you couldn't beat me at a race to the other end of the pond." I smile at him confidently and his eyes sparkle at the challenge.

"Oh you are so on." I take his hand to pull him to a stop and we take our marks.

"Straight across okay?" Adam nods, chuckling as if he thinks he'll beat me. I smile and then swipe his beanie cap from his head. "When the cap falls is when we go."

Adam rubs his hands together in anticipation. "Can we make this interesting?" Adam asks with excitement. I giggle and look at him expectantly so he can go on. "If I win, which I will. You move into my room. If you win...then I'll bring you breakfast in bed until Christmas, but in my bed, though." I laugh.

"Okay...I'll sweeten the deal so you don't try and hold back, if you win, I'll move into your room and I'll throw in a blow job." Adam's eyes widen and he grins like he's won the lottery.

I can't deny that I find the idea of my moving into his room very appealing. Adam is very quickly wiggling his way into my heart and I don't have any rationale to deny it or try to stop it at this point. Adam says it's a deal and there are no take backs. I toss the hat up, as soon as it touches the ice we're off. We're neck in neck for the first few strides and then he starts to slip into the lead. I don't let him get too far ahead before going into overdrive and passing him at the last second.

"What a crushing defeat! I guess you didn't know that

105

our baby sister is a track star, she has that explosive power in her legs."

My spine straightens at the sound of my brother, Trenton's, voice. I turn around and see him and Tristan standing in front of the park bench, all bundled up and smiling as if nothing at all is wrong. My eyes fill with tears and Tristan picks me up off the ice in a bear hug. Trenton wraps his arms around me too in our usual two for one group hug.

"What are you guys doing here?" I ask in shocked disbelief. Too many emotions are surging through me at once and I can't stop the tears from falling.

"We're here to visit our baby sister and the father of our niece or nephew." Trent and Trist set me on my feet and simultaneously their heads swivel around to study Adam who is walking over to us.

My brothers resemble my father a lot. They are both six foot four and have the muscle to fill out their broad shoulders and tall builds. They have largely the same features, strong jaws, light brown hair and skin, curly black hair and even the same dimple in their left cheeks. The only difference is that Trent has my dad's ears and Trist has my mom's.

"Hey guys, it's good to see you in person." My eyebrows rise in surprise Adam called them? Adam shakes my brothers' hands and they continue to scrutinize him a moment longer before Trenton breaks into a grin.

"Of course we'd come. We'll always be grateful that you called to tell us about Ali, otherwise we'd have never known." Tristan says sincerely and I get the urge to hug them both again.

"It was only the right thing to do." Adam says sincerely and Trenton slaps him on the back good-naturedly.

"Good man. So how about we head inside somewhere? I've grown completely desensitized to the snow while living in Cali." Trent shivers and I move to the bench to change my shoes, Adam does the same.

"Ali, you know we have to talk about our parents, right?" Tristan looks at me in all seriousness and I sigh.

"Do we? Can we just ignore their existence and give them what they want? Which is nothing to do with me." Trent shakes his head adamantly.

"No, Ali what they did, how they're acting…its despicable. They need to know that and I want to throw it in their faces. I don't care what your kids do, you don't abandon family." Trent helps me up from the bench and Adam holds my skates as we start to walk back to the house.

"I don't think I'm ready for a confrontation with them. I don't want another confrontation with them. Anyway, they probably won't even acknowledge me." I sigh in defeat.

"They will if they want anything to do with us. We're choosing sides here, mom and dad don't support us anymore. There's nothing they can hold over our heads. We're with you, baby girl." Tristan says simply and in that moment, my love for my brothers nearly overflows. To think that Adam was the one who called them…he really does care for me.

We reach the house and get a fire going in the family room while we all thaw off from the cold.

"So here's the plan. Mom and Dad think we're coming in tonight and we're supposed to go straight there to have dinner and start decorating the tree. You and Adam will come with us and we'll set them straight. If they refuse to stop being so ignorantly blind, then that's that. There's no reaching them." Trenton tells Adam and I what will happen. I wonder if I'm ready to face my parent's like this.

"You think you can handle that, baby girl?" Tristan asks me, picking up on my hesitation. I take a deep breath and simply nod. "There's the strong girl we grew up with. So how about we do some Christmas shopping to occupy our minds before the coming battle, yeah?" Trist stands up and I giggle at the look on Trent's face as he's practically roasting his arms in the fire, trying to get warm.

"Alright, but we're turning the heat up all the way in the car." Trist puts out the fire and the guys get ready to go.

I take the time to pull Adam aside in the front room.

"You called them." I say simply and Adam nods, searching my face, hoping he made the right move. I hug him tightly and whisper in his ear, "thank you."

"I'm just glad you aren't mad at me for doing it."

I shake my head, my eyes threatening to tear up all over again. "Little Bean will have his uncles in his life and even if tonight ends in disaster, I'll never resent you for getting them here."

Adam smiles and he pulls me into his arms again, kissing my temple before letting me go. In this moment, I realize that I love Adam, there was no getting around it and I've finally admitted it to myself. I just wonder if he's realized how he feels yet. He wouldn't have gone to such lengths if he didn't have deep feelings for me.

Chapter 9

Ali's eyes look different. There's no more barrier that I always tried to see past. She's back to being open and expressive, something I fell in love with the moment I spotted her in class. She's finally letting me in and it feels fucking fantastic.

"So who are you going to shop for first?" Ali asks me while slipping her hand into mine as we step into Bloomingdale's. Her brothers have gone off to do 'top secret' shopping on their own.

"My mom. I never know what to get her really. She's always the kind to say, 'all I need is a good card and a kiss, don't spend your money on an old woman.'" Ali laughs fondly, her eyes brighter than I've seen in weeks.

"Alright well...you can never go wrong with perfume or a handbag. Assuming you know what she likes." I look at Ali, at a loss and she laughs at me this time while shaking her head. "Well, I've noticed she needs a new handbag, she said if she had the patience to shop she'd get a nice leather tote, black. Then I was also able to find out that she is running low on her favorite Chanel, which I want to get for her." Ali tells me what to get mom and I could kiss her, in fact I do. Stopping in the middle of foot traffic I press a searing kiss to her lips and smile in satisfaction when I see her pupils have dilated after I pull away.

"Um...maybe I should wait until we're alone to tell

you what your aunt wants for Christmas?" I laugh and we both head into the mall to get to the Neiman Marcus.

After Ali and I get gifts for my family and her brothers, we meet up with Trent and Trist. I leave her to get some lunch with them while I go into Kay Jeweler's to get Ali's gifts and Carter's to get something unisex for Little Bean. I find two outfits I can't choose between, one says 'I love mommy breast' with the word breast crossed out and 'best' written above it. The other says, 'daddy's cool, but mommy has the breasts.' They're funny so I opt for buying both.

"Shit, I wonder how some people can shop all day. Just being here for half the damn day has my eyes crossing." Trenton complains as we all meet up at the brothers' rental truck.

"It's all those bright lights and displays. Long shopping trips aren't meant for men I swear." Tristan agrees with his brother and I can't say I disagree.

"I'm just glad to have gotten everything in one shot." I add.

Ali shakes her head at all of us. "Guys, where's your Christmas spirit? You should be excited about giving everyone their gifts to see what they'll think. I know I got fantastic gifts, all of you will cry when you open yours. I've been saving all year just for Christmas shopping...for good measure, too." She mumbles the last part. Only I hear as I'm sitting in the back with

111

her.

Thinking about what Ali said, I wonder how she'll react to my gifts. I know she'll like the charm bracelet I got her so she can start marking milestones with charms and adding to it. I just have no idea if she'll accept the promise ring I got for her. I know it's too early to ask her to marry me yet, but I want her to know that I fully intend to ask her once we're secure in our love for each other. I guess one could say I'm scared, but I want there to be no hesitation when I ask and when she answers. So when Little Bean asks one day why Ali and I got married I can tell him that it's because I loved her unconditionally and she felt the same way for me.

"Alright folks, let's unload and get ready for this fucking dinner." Trenton announces when we pull up to the house. Ali takes a deep breath and everyone grabs their bags and heads inside.

"Guys, you might have to do rock-paper-scissors for who gets the guest room with the bed in it." Ali informs them and both brothers bolt into the house to stake a claim with their suitcases. "Honestly, they are still children deep down inside." Ali says in fond exasperation.

"Can't take the boy out of the man, you know what they say." I grin and she rolls her eyes.

"I just hope they don't break anything. They are the only twenty-eight year old brothers who still wrestle each other."

I chuckle and shake my head. "You're mistaken about that one Ali. Catch Gabriel and I on a lazy day and you'll see."

She laughs loudly at the visual. Ali and I walk into our bedroom and I close the door behind her. She slips into the closet, probably to hide her Christmas presents and I hide her gifts in the hallway closet. She'll never find it there. The thing it stuffed with building and painting supplies that I've never gotten around to cleaning out.

"Where you going?" I ask her as she passes by me in the direction of her old room.

"I have to get some clothes, don't get your boxers in a bunch." She says with a chuckle in her voice.

I relax with a crooked smile and go ahead into the en-suite to get the shower going. I strip down and step into the stall, letting the warm water cascade over my head. I hear the bathroom door open and close and I smile when I watch Ali strip down to absolutely nothing and join me in the shower. Needless to say we take a bit more time than usual in washing up.

* * *

When we all group up downstairs, Ali is visibly nervous. Trent keeps his arm around her shoulders, stealing my job to comfort her.

"Don't let the anxiety get you, Ali. Let's just do this and get it over with. Whatever happens, happens. Just know that we're with you in the end." Tristan tries to soothe Ali's nerves and I tilt her chin so she can look at me.

"Always. Okay?" I add to Tristan's declaration and she gives a small smile, nodding.

"Alright, let's go." Tristan says and we all pile into their truck again.

I can feel the tension coming off of Ali in waves. We drive out to Westport and a really high-end area of Westport at that. Ali wasn't kidding when she said her parents were successful. The fact that they had a waterfront property spoke volumes. I could see why parents used to the lifestyle they have, would want nothing but excellence from their children.

Trenton pulls into the drive of the large house and turns the car off. Ali takes several deep breaths and then we go out into the cold. Tristan uses his key to get into the house and they walk right in.

"Hello! We're here!" He calls and I take Ali's hand, she follows me in after a moment's hesitation and I reluctantly close the door behind us. I feel like we've just walked into the belly of the beast.

"Oh my boys are here! Finally the family is together…" I recognize Shatrice's voice and when she rounds the corner into the foyer her voice trails off in shock, I just don't know if it's unpleasant shock or not. She looks almost exactly like Ali, just darker in skin tone and her eyes are a darker brown as well.

"What are you doing here?" Shatrice asks Ali, I can tell she wants her voice to come off as forceful, but there is a waver to it that can't be missed.

"We're staying at Ali and Adam's house and we decided to bring them along for dinner, mom." Trenton says without hesitation or pause.

Shatrice's eyes swing over to her sons, her emotions and thoughts unreadable. "Well I can't stop you from staying wherever you want to stay, but it was a mistake to bring them along to a family dinner." Her voice is back to a tone I recognize, she spoke to me the same way when I called her on the phone. My hand tightens around Ali's and I see her chest heave as she drags in a deep breath.

"Last I checked, we were all related here, mom. Ali is our sister and we won't turn our backs on her. Adam is a part of this family too, now." Tristan replies to his mother's insufferable tone in kind and her eyes widen in indignation.

"You better watch how you speak to me, child."

Trenton shakes his head angrily and he steps towards his mother. "That's just the thing isn't mom? We're not children anymore. We're all adults, including Ali. She was being as responsible as any twenty-one year old girl can be, but accidents do happen and we all have to accept it and help her the best we can through this new stage in life."

Shatrice is looking at me now, her eyes are angry, but

what Trenton said got to her and it's plain to see as tears start to fill her gaze. "You did this to her. You ruined her future. Her life didn't have to be this hard and you…you preyed on an innocent student."

"I know I messed up, we both did, but I'm going to spend every day of the rest of my life if I have to making up for it. Ali isn't in this alone."

"What's going on? What are you doing here?" Shawn King walks into the foyer and addresses me directly.

"The boys are staying at Adam's house with Alicia." Is Shatrice's brief explanation.

"You boys would condone this? Whatever is going on between your sister and that teacher?"

Shawn is glancing in between his two sons and they simultaneously get defensive.

Crossing their arms over their chests and widening their stance. "Like we told mom, accidents happen and we refuse to turn our backs on our flesh and blood. If you want to cut Ali and Adam from your lives, not to mention your grandchild, then you're cutting us too." Tristan tells his father in a hard tone, staring him down unflinchingly. Shawn is just as tall and built as his sons, his light brown gaze just as hard.

"Having a child so young is one thing, but having a child out of wedlock is not how we raised you all. This family is not careless or uneducated, so there is no excuse for your sister. This family does not make mistakes, or give birth by accident. If you want to throw your life and career away by getting pregnant, then by all means, do so on your own." The shock hits us all in waves; I don't even think Shatrice was ready for Shawn's words.

"I especially cannot believe you would bring this man into my house after what he's done to Alicia. If you two want to pick sides, we can't stop you. As far as I'm concerned you can all leave." Shawn finishes crisply and turns to leave.

Ali's hand whips out to grip my arm as she's holding her stomach with her other hand and slightly hunched over.

"Ali, what is it, what's wrong?" I hold on to her as she closes her eyes, pain clearly etched into her features. There's a beat of silence as we all look at Ali.

"Has she been eating well? Has she been having bad morning sickness?" Shatrice pulls a one-eighty and shoves Trist and Trent out of the way to tend to Ali.

"Ali, talk to me, tell me what you're feeling so I know how bad it is." Her voice is tender as she speaks to Ali; it's plain to see that she's scared for her daughter.

"I don't know, it's…it's really bad cramping." Ali says weakly. Shatrice moves Ali to sit down on one of the steps of the grand staircase and Ali whimpers.

"It hurts really bad," she says again. I hover around Ali and her mother and suggest anxiously that we should take Ali to the hospital.

"The car is running Shatrice, let's get her outside." Shawn's voice comes from nowhere and I hadn't realized the brothers went to get the truck started. I help Ali into the car and we all pile in, silent while Shawn speeds to the nearest hospital.

"It's going to be alright, don't worry." I try to soothe Ali while rubbing her back; she's still bent over in pain. "I said I'd take care of us, I won't let anything bad happen Ali, don't worry baby." I continue whispering to her and she squeezes my hand. I let her squeeze, she can squeeze my hand until it falls off for all I care, as long as I can comfort her in some way.

We pull into the emergency room entrance of the hospital Ali's mom works at and they take her in right away. Ali is put into a wheelchair and a nurse hurries her into an examination room. I follow beside them, my sole focus on Ali. I don't know what the others do.

"Sir, I'm going to have to ask you to wait with them until we get her all figured out." I shake my head at the nurse.

"No, I'm staying with her. She's pregnant and I'm the father. I have to make sure everything is okay with them."

The nurse hesitates and then sighs, giving in. "Fine,

but you need to stay out of the way of everyone. While we're checking her over."

I nod and watch while he wheels her into room number two and another nurse helps get Ali onto the hospital bed. They ask her questions like, if she has any chronic illnesses, if she's been having worse than normal morning sickness, under too much stress, any family medical history. All while another nurse gets Ali's pants off and they drape her to be examined. I stand over by Ali's head and hold her hand.

"It's gonna be alright, who knows, it's probably just indigestion." I smile at Ali and she tries to smile in return, it looks more like a grimace.

Quicker than I could've expected an ultra sound machine is wheeled into the room and a doctor is informing Ali that they are going to do a vaginal ultrasound to check on the baby.

"Okay, so the good news is that the babies look perfectly healthy, you can see their heartbeats there…" The doctor points to the screen and sure enough I see two little beans. Not one…but two, with two flashing white pulsations signifying their heartbeats. Ali's jaw drops and I simply stare at the screen. They are healthy, they are safe…there's a they…we're having twins?

"The other news is that you had a threatened miscarriage, there was some blood, but luckily not too much was lost." The doctor finally glances up at Ali and I and she smiles lopsidedly.

"I take it this is the first time you two are hearing the word twins?" Ali and I nod in tandem. "Well congratulations. So after we get some paperwork done, you will be discharged. I demand you go straight home and get into bed. Rest for a few days, no heavy lifting, and no sex. After about a week, you can have a follow up appointment with your OB and she'll advise you from there." The doctor talks at Ali, but her eyes are practically glazed over from shock.

After the room empties of nurses and the doctor, Trenton, Tristan, Shatrice and Shawn walk in a moment later.

"So what happened? Is everything okay?" Trenton is eyeing Ali worriedly and after taking in the look on her face they all look to me to explain. Because apparently I look more coherent than she does.

"It was a threatened miscarriage, Ali has to rest for a few days and follow up with her OB…they did an ultrasound and…we now have two babies instead of one growing in there."

Shatrice gasps, her eyes filling with tears. Trent and Trist actually find it exciting and hug and kiss Ali. Shawn's expression goes from unreadable to misty. He takes a deep breath and wipes a hand over his face.

"This is almost exactly how we found out your mom was going to have twins when she was pregnant with the boys…she almost lost them, but they weren't going anywhere." He says softly.

Ali finally looks up at him and he takes a deep shuddering breath. "I'm sorry Ali…I'm sorry. The boys are right…you're right. We shouldn't turn our backs on you. It's just that we got…scared, we were so shocked that we didn't know how to react…" Shawn's voice wavers and he trails off.

"We only want the best for you and it felt as if we couldn't help you have the best life anymore."

Ali looks between both parents, her expression guarded and confused. "You…you both said all those hurtful things to me. Being scared for my future is one thing, but completely turning your backs on me is another." Ali's voice starts small, but builds in strength. Her suppressed hurt and anger coming to the surface.

"We handled this all wrong, yes…we said despicable things to you baby, but we can figure things out, we'll help you get on your feet. I'm just so sorry baby. I should have never said those things to you." Shatrice asks for forgiveness from Ali and unshed tears spill over to her cheeks.

"I agree with your mother, we just want you safe and happy. I'm sorry for speaking so harshly to you, sorry that we caused you so much pain that could've caused you to lose your babies." Shawn is sincere, it's clear to see in his misty-eyed gaze, as he looks lovingly into his daughter's eyes. He was just a man, afraid for his daughter, one who doesn't deal with stress well at all.

"Anything you need baby, we'll be there. We want to be in your life, in the babies' lives…" Shatrice adds earnestly. They may want to mend bridges with Ali, but it's becoming clear that they don't hold me in as much esteem as Trenton and Tristan do.

"Please Ali, just tell us we're forgiven." Shawn moves to Ali's other side to take her hand and I reluctantly relinquish my spot on Ali's other side so Shatrice can do the same.

"So…you didn't actually mean all those things you said?" Ali looks from Shawn to Shatrice and back. The fact that Ali is willing, hoping in fact, to forgive them, speaks volumes about her character. She's just so fucking perfect and she keeps getting better.

"No Ali, that was pain and confusion speaking through us. We should've taken the time to accept all of this, but instead we handled it horribly." Ali's mom holds onto her daughter's hand tightly and Ali promptly bursts into tears.

"I forgive you. I never wanted my baby -- my babies to grow up without their grandparents in their lives." Shawn and Shatrice hug Ali tightly, it's plain to see the love they all have for each other and I finally breathe a sigh of relief.

"You did it, man." Trent claps my shoulder and smiles at me with respect in his eyes. "If it wasn't for you, well, who knows where we'd be now." I shrug and can't help but think that if it weren't for me, Ali wouldn't have gone through all she had during the past eight weeks.

"I just made sure we got everyone together."

Tristan shakes his head and then glances at the three still hugging, Ali and her mother still crying as well.

"No you fixed something deeper than that. Forced it to the surface and it's being mended right in front of us." Tristan inclines his head towards me, his expression grateful.

The Final Chapter

Two days after my trip to the hospital, I can say I never want to be on bed rest ever again. Though it's incredibly nice to have Adam cater to me, the hovering of all our family is getting to be a little much. Not that I wouldn't trade it for the world. I just don't want to have to go through it again when I'm in my last trimester.

"Ali, your mom and mama Lina are having a disagreement for what color the babies room should be. Lina says a buttercup yellow; your mom says a soft blue. Honestly I can't take much more of their banter. Meanwhile, the men are having a debate about how much money fast food chains spend on attorneys. Gabriel's wife Eve is trying to get them out of the kitchen because in about three minutes aunt Ania will hit one of them over the head with a hot pan as she's trying to cook and they keep eating everything before it can be made." Kelsey takes a deep breath after rattling off another report.

"That's why I played the 'resting' card and came in here to hide out. I've got Oreos, you want some?" I offer Kels some cookies and she climbs into bed with me.

"I'm so happy that Little Bun is back on the table though. It's so much better than Little Bean." I giggle and roll my eyes.

"They are practically the same name Kelsey." She snorts and whispers that her name is better under her breath.

"Hey, what are you two doing in here?" Adam walks into the bedroom and smiles, that familiar twinkle in his eye. He looks as if he's a bit pleased with himself.

"I should ask you that? What have you been up to?"

Adam climbs into bed with Kelsey and I, squeezing into the middle and stealing the box of Oreos for himself.

"Well I've just been thinking that maybe I should become a firefighter. The hours are flexible and I'm really good at it." Both Kelsey and I look at him as if he's lost it.

"Adam you don't even like to get close to the oven." I remind him and Kelsey laughs at his quirk.

"Well I was being metaphoric anyway. I settled the great paint debate. We're going for a blue and yellow nursery and then I successfully proved that fast food chains don't spend the most on lawyers, department stores do. Aunt Ania is no longer threatening anyone with hot oil. Now everyone is watching a movie downstairs so I've come to get you."

"Oh! I brought caramel popcorn, I'll go and make a batch." Kelsey heads downstairs and I take the moment we have alone to kiss Adam.

"Hey now, if you keep that up it'll be really hard to stick to doctor's orders," Adam says after I run my tongue along his bottom lip.

"Adam, I never thanked you for getting my family back together…I really-I…I love you." The words insert themselves without my conscious decision to tell him how I feel and Adam's eyes widen with pleasure before the most breathtaking smile spreads across his features.

"I love you too, Ali. More than life itself, I'd do anything for your happiness." Adam is staring intently into my eyes and there's no question that he's sincere, he really means what he just said.

My eyes fill with water and I throw my arms around his neck. I don't think my heart has ever felt so full before. "So what do you say we head downstairs and watch that movie?" Adam picks me up easily and he makes his way towards the bed.

"What movie are we watching?" I ask and he grins at me boyishly.

"Finding Nemo."

I giggle and can't help but kiss him again. "Really? Gabriel and my brothers and everyone agreed to watch Finding Nemo?"

"No, of course not. We're watching White Christmas." I laugh and smack Adam lightly on the chest.

"She can walk you know, Adam." My mom points this out as we round the corner into the family room. Everyone is cozied up around the TV and fireplace.

"I know, but I don't want her to do too much yet when she doesn't have to." Adam sets me down on the couch and I snuggle in between my dad and brother Trent.

Looking around the room with all my family, old and new, I have to say I'm perfectly content in this moment. Adam glances up at me from his spot on the floor and flashes me another sexy smile. Yeah, he's pretty perfect, too.

THE END

THE END

Message From The Author:

Hiii

I really hope you enjoyed "**Her Teacher's Baby**".

As you bought the special edition of this book you now have a FREE bonus book to enjoy starting on the next page entitled "**The Sheikh's Reluctant Bride**".

I hope you enjoy that one too!

Cherry x x

BONUS BOOK

THE SHEIKH'S RELUCTANT BRIDE

CHERRY KAY

About This Book:

When Sara is photographed in a compromising situation with Sheikh Raphael they both find it awkward.
However, Sheikh Raphael finds it so awkward that he believes the only way to save his honor is by marrying her and telling the world she is his wife.

And Raphael approaches her offering her an obscene amount of money to marry him for a short period of time she finds it hard to say no and she reluctantly agrees.

But she has no idea what she let herself in for...

THE SHEIKH'S RELUCTANT BRIDE

Chapter One

Sara hurried out of the bus, clutching her bag. She glanced at her watch as she ran down the street. She had only three minutes left to get to her interview with Salam Oils & Gasses. It was one of the best oil companies. She wanted to work there after she graduated, however, life had not gone the way she planned.

Even though she was going to interview for an administrative job, it was not her dream, but it was okay. She needed to do whatever she could to support her family. Sara checked both sides of the road before she entered the big, intricately built structure. She checked the time once more.

As she was running, clumsy as always, she tripped herself. Her hands flew in the air, trying to grab hold onto something but she had no such luck. Just when she almost hit the ground, an arm reached out to hold onto her. She grabbed onto something and held tightly. She looked up and saw a very tall, handsome man with beautiful almond skin color looking down at her. Sara couldn't help but stare into his midnight black eyes.

"Are you okay?" He helped her up to her feet. His voice was so deep, it gave her goosebumps. She realized that as he was catching her, he had actually grabbed her bottom. She wiggled out of his embrace and took a step back. Now that she was standing upright, she immediately noticed how tall he was. Her head reached his collarbone, and she was in heels. "Watch where you are touching," she said to him. He just stared at her with a blank facial expression. She shifted awkwardly "I am fine, thank you," Sara replied quietly. She tucked a curly lock of hair behind her ear. She had put her hair into a bun, but she always seemed to miss the lock by her ear.

He still wasn't saying anything. He was just looking at her chest with a blank facial expression.

"What?" Sara asked him. She followed his gaze. She gasped so loudly when she realized that she had lost two buttons. How could that happen? It was bad enough to lose one, but two? Only she could pull off something like that.

"Oh no!" How could that be happening to her? Yes, the shirt she was wearing was quite old, but why did it tear now, right before her interview. She placed her hands on her chest to try to cover herself. Her black lace bra was showing and this man could see it. He took his suit jacket off and placed it on her shoulders. She felt awkward, standing there with this random man dressing her in his expensive jacket. She caught his scent when he was near her, he smelled really nice.

"You do not want people seeing your assets," he said.

"Thank you." She caught a quick glance at his watch. "Oh, no," she cried out and just ran off. It was the time of her interview and she could not afford to be late. She needed that job. She rushed into the building and approached the reception desk.

The receptionist ushered Sara into the large conference room. There was a panel of four people ready to interview her. They sat at a mahogany table in their expensive suits looking at her with stern faces.

***

"Sheikh, sheikh!" Malik cried out hysterically as he rushed into Sheikh Raphael's office. The sheikh was sitting at his desk doing work, as usual. He looked up casually.

"What is it?" He looked at his overly dramatic assistant. He had a tendency of overreacting at the very smallest of matters.

"Look at this." Malik placed the Egyptian Times on the desk in front of the sheikh. Raphael picked up the newspaper and read the headlines; *Who is Sheikh Raphael's woman?*

Raphael lowered his eyebrows as he glared at the photographs. There was one of him with his hand grabbing onto the woman's bottom. From the angle it was taken, it looked as though they were quite intimate. The other photo was of him dressing her in his jacket. In the photograph, the woman was gazing at him as if she was about to kiss him. Of course, the tabloids would speculate about their relationship.

It was the woman he had run into when he had visited Dallas. He still remembered how clumsy she had been. She was lucky that he had been there to catch her; otherwise, she would have had a nasty fall. To make the situation that much more awkward for the both of them, her buttons had fallen off, revealing her hazelnut colored breasts sitting high on her chest.

"This is a problem," said Sheikh Raphael.

"Yes, it is," replied his assistant. "There are blogs suggesting that she is a secret lover." Malik paused and just looked at the sheikh awkwardly.

"I do not know her." Raphael already knew that Malik wanted to ask him who she was. "I was just helping her, and of course the paparazzi would photograph us at such a moment."

"The timing is very bad."

Raphael nodded. The last thing he needed was a scandal. He had lived a very private life. He had never been involved in any scandals. There had been a few articles questioning why he was thirty-two years old and not married.

Now that he was replacing his father as the head of the Salam Organization, he needed every aspect of his life to be perfect. The Salam Organization had been formed by his grandfather and other sheikhs decades ago. It had joined tribes and cities in Egypt. The sheikhs from each city or tribe had signed the peace treaty. The Organization was also in charge of the country's natural oils and gasses.

The other sheikhs were already doubting whether Raphael was old enough to be the head. He was thirty-two years old, and he could not afford to let a scandal give them more reasons to not appoint him as the head sheikh.

"I have to get to this woman before anyone else does." said Raphael. By anyone, he meant Sheikh Hosny. The man was cunning. He watched Raphael's every move, waiting for him to make a mistake. He wanted to be the head of Salam Organization.

"If they get to her, she will deny knowing you," said Malik.

"That will not help anything. She could be bought to do anything they want from her."

"That is very true. I will start looking for her."

Raphael nodded. "The sooner the better."

"But what will you do when you find her?"

"I could pay for her silence but her face is already out there. This won't stop the speculations and rumors." Raphael had been caught in a compromising situation and knew that ignoring the situation would not help. Reporters were definitely going to ask him about it. Even if he explained the situation, no one would believe him. That was the worst thing about the media. They could spin anything into a scandal.

"I will just have to marry her," said Sheikh Raphael as he leaned back in his chair.

*

"Miss Pierce!" Sara heard a voice calling out from behind her, as she walked home.

She turned her head and saw a man dressed in an expensive looking suit approaching her. He did not look like someone she would know.

"Who's asking?"

"I am Malik Khan and I have been sent here to speak with you by my boss."

Sara frowned. "And who is your boss?"

"The man in this photo with you." Malik handed the Egyptian Times to Sara.

"What is this?" She crossed her eyebrows and looked at the newspaper. She saw a picture of herself and the man that had caught her from falling. She gasped and stopped walking. "Why would this be in the

135

newspaper? An Egyptian newspaper at that?" She looked at Malik and waited for answers.

"Is there somewhere we could sit and talk? It is a matter of confidentiality." He spoke with a Middle Eastern accent, and he spoke eloquently. Sara nodded and quickly led him into a café. She could not wait to hear what this was all about.

She sat down at one of the tables. Malik waited for her to sit down first before he joined her.

"Well, who is your boss and why did he send you to me?" She was curious to know why the paparazzi would photograph him and her together.

"Sheikh Raphael Tadros," Said Malik.

"Who is he?"

Malik raised his eyebrows. He seemed surprised by her question. "You do not know the sheikh?"

"No, I do not."

"Oh." He did not seemed pleased.

"So he is a sheikh? And that is why I was photographed with him?"

"Yes."

"And it was such an awkward picture." Sara laughed a little. It was a very weird situation for her. What were the chances that she would be pictured with a sheikh? "So why did he send you over?"

"He would like to speak with you."

"When and why?"

"This picture, being in tabloids, will be detrimental to his reputation; he needs to speak to you about it. He will be in town in two days."

"So he wants to discuss a picture."

"Miss Pierce, it is an important matter."

Sara sighed. "I have a lot of things to do. I cannot just take time out to meet with him."

"Any time and all time you spend with him will be compensated."

"Why can't you tell me what he needs to speak to me about? I mean I understand that this picture can cause rumors for a man of his stature, but what does he expect me to do about it?"

"This is an issue that will cause more than just rumors." He pulled out a document out of his briefcase and passed it to Sara. "So between now and when you meet with the sheikh, you cannot speak to anyone about this. So if you could sign this document."

"Sign what?" Sara frowned. She picked up the document and started reading it. She burst out laughing. "You want me to sign a non-disclosure agreement?"

"It is imperative that you do." Malik was so serious. Sara shook her head.

"I do not plan to speak to anyone, nor do I have the time." She slid the document back to him. She was definitely not going to sign anything.

"I would appreciate it if you would sign the agreement."

"Take my word for it."

"Miss Pierce-"

"I am not signing it." Sara was standing her ground on that issue. "When do I meet this sheikh?"

Malik sighed. "We will send a car for you in two days."

"I can make my own way."

Malik was silent for a moment. "Okay." He pulled a business card and wrote an address on the back of it. He gave it to Sara.

"Thank you." Sara took the card and slipped it in her bag.

***

Two days had passed and it was time for Sara to meet with this so-called sheikh. The whole situation was rather strange for her. A Middle Eastern man popped out of the blue and approached her with a non-disclosure agreement. She could not understand why he was making such a big deal out of this photograph. She decided to go to meet this sheikh. She was curious to hear what he had to say to her. Sara walked into Hotel Crescent Court, a place she would normally never go. It was far too expensive and luxurious for her. Malik was waiting for her in the hotel lobby.

"Good evening, Miss Pierce. You came later than we expected."

"I had to work," Sara replied. She was still in her work clothes and her curly hair was a little messy. She knew she was not all that presentable, but she did not have the time to change.

"This way." Malik led her into the elevator. They stopped at the top floor, the presidential suite.

Sara stood on the cream carpet and gaped at the luxurious room. It was large and filled with expensive furniture. "The sheikh is on the balcony."

"Okay." She nodded and followed him. She clutched onto her bag. She had a rape alarm and pepper spray in her bag, just in case. She walked out onto the balcony with Malik. There was a man sitting there reading some documents and drinking whiskey. Sara instantly recognized him from when he caught her.

"Sheikh," Malik said and bowed his head. "Miss Pierce has arrived."

"You may leave us," said Raphael. Malik bowed and left immediately.

"Sit down," he said to Sara. She raised her eyebrows. She was not fond of people commanding her. Raphael looked up.

"Are you asking me?" Sara asked him.

"Would you like to sit down?" He rephrased his statement.

"Yes, thank you." Sara sat down.

"Whiskey? Or would you like something else?"

"No, thank you. I do not drink alcohol."

Raphael raised his eyebrows. He studied Sara for a moment. She was not well put together, the way he preferred his women. She had smooth dark skin with no make-up on. She was not that tall, just over five feet three inches tall. She had an interesting hourglass shape figure."You refused to sign the non-disclosure agreement," he said, getting straight to the point.

"I did not feel that there was a need to do so," she replied. "Who was I going to talk to? And what would I say, anyway?"

She looked confused.

"Someone might approach you to ask the nature of our relationship."

Sara laughed. "There is no relationship." He studied her as she spoke.

"Let me get to the point. This picture is damaging to my reputation. Also, there will be people that will

139

come after you, and pay you to say whatever they need you to say."

"I am not a liar."

"At the right price anyone can be."

"What do you want from me?"

"You were heading into Salam Oils & Gasses."

"Yes, and?"

Raphael did not like how she spoke to him. Women should have more manners and respect than what she was displaying.

"You need a job to support your family."

Sara frowned. "What does that have to do with you?"

"I can help you with whatever you need for your family."

"Who said that my family needs help?"

"Your mother needs surgery and radiation but she does not have health insurance."

"You did a background check on me? How dare you?" Sara immediately got into defense mode. She rose from her seat.

"I have to know who I am dealing with," Raphael said calmly. He gestured for Sara to sit down but she ignored it.

"You have no right getting into my business."

"I can help you, if you help me."

"You sick man. You want to play with my mother's life."

"The opposite actually. I am willing to get her the best medical care possible, and get your siblings into good schools."

"For what in exchange?"

"Marriage."

"Excuse me?"

"Marry me."

Chapter 2

"What?" Sara called out. She frowned at Raphael. He could that she was confused. "Marry you? Does that even make sense?"

"Like I said, help me and I will help you."

"You are crazy." Sara headed for the door as fast as she could. Raphael was not into playing cat and mouse but he was not going to let Sara walk out without him convincing her. He followed her and caught her arm before she left. "Let go --- of me!" she cried out.

"I will not let the compromising photos and rumors tarnish my reputation," he said to her. "Hear me out."

"Just explain what happened and move on with your life. That will be easier."

"It will not. There are people are who eager to witness my downfall. All they need is a small thing like this to happen. Then they start paying women to say that they were my lovers and falsely accusing me for many transgressions."

"Is it really that big of a deal?"

"Yes, damn it!" Raphael was getting frustrated. He had never had to explain himself to anyone. "I am going to be the CEO of Salam Oils & Gasses. A scandal regarding myself and many female lovers is against the moral code. Which means that I will not be able to take office."

Sara's eyes widened. "You are the CEO of Salam Oils & Gasses?" she asked.

"My father is at the moment but he is going to retire next month. Nothing can go wrong between now and then." He could not believe how much information he had just blurted out to Sara. It was very much unlike him but she was stubborn and it was frustrating.

"I understand your predicament, but how can I just marry you?"

"It will be temporary. Only until I have taken office and have settled in to the position."

"I don't know." Sara shook her head. "I can't do it."

"Think about your mother's health. Nothing is more important."

"Stop talking about my mother."

"I can have her admitted into a great medical facility just by the snap of my finger. It is up to you."

Raphael let go of her. "I am here for another day. You have twenty-four hours. When you have reached a decision, come back here same time tomorrow and let me know."

"Why so soon?"

"Because the longer this matter is unattended to, the more time there is for other people to find you. And it would be better for your mother to get her surgery as soon as possible." Raphael turned on his heel and headed into another room. She'd told herself that he was crazy, that she was not going to take him up on his offer. However, when she walked in on her mother examining her breasts, she immediately started worrying over her. Her mother tried to act as if she was okay, but Sara could see how scared she was. So, the next evening, Sara found herself standing outside Raphael's door. Sara took a deep breath and knocked on the door. Malik opened the door. He wore that same strict uptight look on his face. "Good evening, Miss Pierce. Please, come in."

"Thank you." Sara walked in. Raphael was sitting on the sofa wearing a white shirt and black trousers.

"Good evening, Miss Pierce," he said without looking up from the laptop. Sara made herself comfortable on the sofa opposite him.

"How would this work, exactly?"

Raphael closed the laptop and put it on the sofa next to him. He looked at Sara with a blank facial expression. Sara felt no warmth from him. How could she be married to such man? Even if it was a contract marriage, they needed to at least get along.

"You and I will wed. Small ceremony, private. We will be married for at least six months and then we divorce," he said plainly. Sara was pleased that he wanted a small ceremony. The last thing she wanted was a big wedding splashed on the news.

"That's it?"

Raphael nodded at Malik. He approached Sara with a non-disclosure agreement. "Please sign." Sara hesitated, raising her brows again. "Another agreement."

"It is imperative."

Sara sighed before she started reading the agreement. It was basically stating that the marriage between them was to last no more than six months, but the time would be extended if there was an emergency situation. Neither Sara nor Raphael was allowed to let a third party know that it was a contract marriage. Sara's mother was to receive all medical care necessary, and Sara was to receive a hefty financial incentive.

Sara sighed, and signed the contract. She always thought that when she got married, she would at least be in love with the groom, and not marry for money. However, she was going to do everything in her power to help her family. Her mother and her little sisters needed her.

"Excellent," said Raphael.

Malik handed Sara a small black velvet box.

"What is this?" she asked as she analyzed the box before opening it. She gasped when she saw what was inside.

"You will need to wear it," he commanded her once again. It was apparent to Sara that Raphael was not one to ask for anything.

"What?" Sara asked. She was in shock. She had never seen a ring so beautiful in her life. It was an engagement ring. A square shaped blue sapphire sat in the middle of the silver band. There were small, neatly cut diamonds encompassing the sapphire. Sara knew nothing about jewelry but she knew that it was expensive.

She looked at Raphael. "I can't take this. It's too much." She had never liked accepting gifts from men. Now, she was having to accept a ring far more expensive than anything she had ever been offered.

"You have to. The press will question why you do not wear your ring if we are engaged."

"But it..." Sara could not make out a sentence. The ring was too extravagant.

"Now that we are clear on that, I have to leave tonight. I have matters to attend to. I assume you have loose ends to tie, so you may follow in a few days."

And he was right. Sara had to quit her job and make sure that her family was okay. She could not believe what she was doing, but she'd signed the contract.

There was no turning back. She slipped the ring into her bag.

**

Raphael made good on his promise. All of Sara's mother's medical care had already been paid and arranged. Sara's mother kept asking her where she had gotten the money. Her reply was that her new job in Egypt offered medical insurance. She didn't know how to tell her mother why she was going to Egypt.

Three days after Sara signed the contract, a car was sent to pick her up. She was glad that she was leaving after knowing that her mother was getting the treatment she needed. The money she was going to get from the marriage was enough for a deposit on a new house and to look after her little sisters.

The car took her to the airport. She did not have to check in or anything. She was taken to the private jet that was waiting for her. For a moment, she stood there just staring at it. She had never been in one.

"Please come in," the flight attendant said to her with a smile on her face. Sara looked at the sapphire on her finger. She took a deep breath and marched up the stairs and into the jet.

She glanced at the interior as she entered. It was as if she was in an expensive suite. She had not expected it to look like that. She sat in the white leather chair with a red cushion on it. There was the option of sitting on sofas. The carpet was brown and matched the other leather chair.

"Would you like to have anything to eat or drink?" the flight attendant asked her.

"No, thank you." Sarah looked behind her. There was a designated eating area with a white table with silver legs. There were two white leather chairs with brown backs at the table. The jet was simply amazing.

"Okay. If you would just like to buckle your seatbelt. We will be taking off in a few minutes."Sara nodded and did as told.

Chapter Three

Sara waited inside Raphael's living room about twelve hours later. She arrived at 10pm. She nervously waited inside the spacious room with the high ceilings. The floor was made of different colored marble, arranged elegantly to form interesting patterns.

There was a golden chandelier hanging from the ceiling. There was a cream and gold fireplace on the extreme left side of the room. In front of it was blue sofa with brown cushions on it, and there were two single brown chairs opposite the blue sofa.

"You made it."

Sara heard someone speak before she was finished observing the living room. She turned her head towards the voice and saw Raphael walking down the carpeted stairs. He was wearing a sky blue shirt and black trousers. His hair was cut with short in the back and the sides. His beard looked a few days old. Sara admitted to herself that he looked good, but she wondered if he ever dressed casually.

"I did."

"I trust that your flight was pleasant." His voice was low and alluring.

"It was fine, thank you. Now I am just tired."

"I shall show you to your room." Raphael turned on his heel and headed up the stairs. Sara followed.

"My room? So that means I will not be sharing with you?" Sara had been wondering about that. Raphael turned to look at her.

"Were you hoping to share my bed?" he asked with a plain facial expression.

"No." Sara looked away. She had hoped for the opposite.

"I see you wore the ring."

"Well, who knows who I was going to meet on my way here?"

"You did well." His words were a verbal pat on the head. He had addressed her as if she were a child.

They walked up the stairs and headed down the wide corridor. They passed maids on their way to her room. Each maid greeted Raphael with a bow. Sara was fascinated with everything. It was a whole new world to her.

"Here we are," said Raphael when they had reached her bedroom. Sara wanted to gasp and glare, but she held it together. The room was simply amazing. It was five times bigger than her room in Dallas. She shared it with her little sisters.

"This whole accommodation is mine?" Sara asked.

"It is. You may rest tonight; I shall speak with you in the morning. Call on the maids should you need anything." Raphael left the room. Sara frowned. He had no warmth in his voice and he was not all that welcoming. He made it clear that their relationship was strictly business.

Sara sighed. She noticed her suitcase in the bedroom. One of the maids must have come upstairs with it earlier. She opened it and searched for her pajamas. She slipped into them before she climbed into the four-poster king sized bed.

Despite being in a new environment, Sara slept like a baby. Of course she did, especially since she was lying on silk sheets and had so many pillows on the bed. She loved pillows.

In the morning, she climbed out of bed and went to take a shower in her walk-in shower. Maybe life as sheikh's wife was not going to be so bad, she thought to herself.

She slung her long, thick, tight coils of hair into a messy ponytail. Then she put on a loose top and jeans. She headed downstairs for breakfast. She got a little bit lost on her way to the dining room, so she had to ask the maids for directions.

Sara slowly walked into the large dining room with marble flooring. There was round table in the middle of the room big enough for no more than eight people. There was an unusual golden chandelier hanging just above the table.

Raphael was already sitting at the table, reading a newspaper. Sara's face brightened when she saw the long side dining table with lots of different foods on it. She was famished. She pulled out the chair and sat down.

"I trust that you slept well?" he asked her, without putting the newspaper down.

"Shouldn't you look at people when you speak to them?" Sara asked. She had noticed that he never properly greeted her nor did he stop what he was doing when she arrived. He always acted like that with her. It was rude.

"I do as I please."

Sara rolled her eyes. He was arrogant. She poured herself some orange juice, without answering Raphael. She took a sip of it, and it tasted delightful..

"I have an itinerary for you." Raphael folded his newspaper and put it on the table.

"Excuse me?"

A house cleaner placed a document next to Sara. She narrowed her gaze at it. Raphael had an obsession with documents/contracts, she thought to herself. She picked up the itinerary and started reading it. She started laughing uncontrollably.

"What is amusing?" Raphael asked her calmly. He shoved some eggs in his mouth as he waited for her response.

"This list is amusing," Sara replied. He was crazy if he thought that she was going to do all that. It never stated that she had to do all that in the contract.

"I cannot see what is amusing about it."

"Etiquette lessons?"

"Yes, a sheikh's wife must carry herself in a particular manner."

Sara was in disbelief. "Arabic lessons?"

"That is quite obvious. You must speak Arabic."

"Who said I don't?"

"Do you?"

"I do not, but that is beside the point."

"What is the point?"

Sara frowned and put the list down. "You are demanding too much of me. You did not even ask about my opinion in regards to all of this."

"Like I said, being a sheikh's wife--"

"Means you have to carry yourself in a particular way?" Sara interjected.

"Yes, and you have to look a certain way also..."

"What is wrong with the way I look?"

"For starters, your hair is unkempt."

"Excuse me?" Sara put her fork down. Raphael was really being rude and controlling. It was uncalled for.

If he thought that she could easily be controlled, then he had another thing coming.

"Secondly, your clothing is unacceptable." He spoke calmly, and ignoring her obvious distaste.

"This is ridiculous."

"I beg to differ."

Raphael wiped his mouth with the napkin and rose from his seat. "I have to be at the office," he said to Sara.

"Go, and just know that I will not be doing anything from this damned list."

"Picking a fight against me is futile. You might as well give up and just make things easier for yourself."

He walked out of the room.

Chapter Four

Sara didn't even have the opportunity to say anything to Raphael before he just walked out. It was not the first time he had done that to her, she hated it. He was actually rude and cold. It did not surprise her, she expected rich people to behave in that manner. Sara got up from the dining table and went back to *her* room.

She looked around as she headed back upstairs. Raphael's house was quite impressive. Never had she ever imagined living in such a house. Living as a sheikh's wife was going to be harder than she thought. He had different ideas about the type of wife she was going to be. She thought that she was just going to be his wife and then go.

The maids really stared and studied Sara as she walked by. Some of them whispered amongst themselves and quickly stopped when Sara looked. She knew what they were talking about. It was clear that they were curious about Sara and Raphael's relationship.

Sara walked into her room. It resembled a hotel room, a very expensive one. There was a beige sofa by the windows. The color of the sofa matched the curtains. Sara approached it. Just as she was about to sit down, there was a knock on the door.

"Come in." She called out. She assumed that it was one of the maids.

To her surprise, it was not. An older but elegant looking woman walked into the room. She was dressed in a white tube skirt and a long sleeved white shirt. It had tiny neat pleats in the middle, from the neck down to the stomach. Her jet-black hair was pinned up into a bun.

"Good morning, Miss Pierce."

"Hello." Sara slowly walked towards her.

"I am Mariam, Raphael's aunt."

"Nice to meet you."

Mariam looked at Sara from head to toe and then back up. Sara was starting to feel a little bit awkward. Mariam was clearly studying her. She walked over to the coffee table that was set opposite to the four-poster bed. There were three beige chairs around the table. Mariam put her bag on the table.

"We have a lot of work to do," said Mariam.

Sara looked at her questioningly.

"Work?" She was confused.

"Yes. Raphael told me to come and work with you."

Ahh, now it made sense, Sara thought to herself. She was the one who was going to give her etiquette lessons and Arabic lessons.

"Did he?" Sara asked. She wondered how she was going to decline her help in a respectful manner. She never wanted to disrespect an older person.

"Yes, he did. Let us start with something simple. Show me how you walk." She spoke so eloquently with so much poise.

"Did he not tell you that I was not going to partake in anything?"

"It is mandatory," said Mariam. Mandatory? The word echoed in Sara's head. This was not school. She was an adult. "Raphael is a sheikh and as a sheikh's wife, you must portray yourself in a certain manner. One simple mistake and the press will get a hold of it and turn it into something that will taint his image."

"What exactly about me needs changing?" Sara did not like being told that she was not good enough, that there was work to be done on her image. She was fine with the way she looked and acted.

"You need to speak Arabic, at least at a basic level," said Mariam. Her gaze lingered over Sara's hair. "Your hair could use some taming."

"Taming." Sara repeated. Why did her hair need taming? Granted her hair was messy at the time but she was at home, it was not as if she was out with Raphael.

"You have lovely curls." Sara smiled but she knew Mariam was going to say more about it.

"You will just need a more elegant look."

Sara sighed. As much as she wanted to protest against Mariam, she could not. This contract marriage was going to benefit her family. She had to pick her battles.

"I see."

"For now I would like to see how you walk and just work on your posture."

When Sara started walking, Mariam immediately showed displeasure. Sara never thought that there was anything wrong with the way she was walking. Mariam stopped Sara and told her to walk a bit slower. Moments later, she told her not to drag her feet.

They spent hours working on Sara's walk. Mariam even demonstrated how to walk like a proper lady. Sara tried to imitate but she was unsuccessful.

"The way you walk speaks volumes about yourself. You need to look confident and graceful," said

Mariam. It made Sara wonder what her walk portrayed.

After hours of teaching Sara how to walk in a straight line, at the right pace and not swing her arms so much, Mariam showed Sara how to sit properly. She told Sara not to slouch or hunch when she sat down. She also showed her how to greet people. She wasn't to shake hands with men or kiss them on the cheek unless they were related to Raphael.

Sara was really happy when Mariam left. Working with her had been so exhausting. Mariam was strict and relentless. She made Sara repeat the same thing repeatedly, no matter how long it took. Raphael was going to pay for this.

**

Sara lay in her bed, flicking through TV channels. Sadly, Raphael had been working late, so he had not come for dinner. She dined alone. She enjoyed the food, though. Her little sisters would have enjoyed it. She wished that she could have shared all this good food with them.

In her baggy pajama bottoms and over-sized t-shirt, Sara got out of bed and went for a walk around the house. She still had not seen the house in its entirety. She walked out of her room and continued down the hall. The maids greeted her as she walked past them. Sara wondered to herself if Raphael had told them she was his wife to be.

Sara took a turn when she reached the end of the corridor. At the end of that corridor, there was a huge door. She pushed the door open and into a large fancy living room with marble flooring. There were low white sofas with black cushions. Sara walked in and just looked around. There were paintings hung up on the walls. She was not into paintings, so she could not guess the artists. She walked out of the living room and down the hall.

"What are you doing here?" She heard Raphael's voice. She turned to her left, where the voice was coming from. There were glass doors wide open, revealing a neat office. Raphael was sitting at the desk.

"Just looking around. What is this place?" she asked him as she walked in.

"My chambers."

Sara raised her eyebrows. Who referred to their bedroom as chambers? Granted, he had an office and a living room, so you could not exactly call his private space a bedroom.

"So you came from work to do more work?"

"I stay on top of all things." Raphael put his pen down and leaned back in his seat. His gaze washed over Sara.

"What?" She asked him.

"Are you really walking around the house looking like that?"

"Like what?"

"The hair, the clothes"

Sara frowned. "I do not need to dress up to go to bed." She said.

"You sleep like this?"

"Raphael!" she called out. "You asked me to marry you, not the other way round. So take me as I am and stop trying to change me."

"You call me by my name," he said as he rose from his seat.

"What else?" She noticed that a few buttons on shirt were undone, revealing his chest.

"Sheikh," He said as he approached her. Sara laughed.

"If you are going to be my husband, why would I still call you sheikh?

Her husband. It was weird for her to say. He stopped right in front of her and just stared down at her. He was so much taller than she was. He was quite muscular, which made his physique intimidating.

"Your husband," he said. Sara was feeling awkward. His chest was distracting her. She had to say something, fast!

"I met your aunt today."

"I am aware."

"I think we covered enough. No more lessons needed." That was not it. She wanted to thank him for sending her and yet she did not. Damn his chest!

"Is that so?"

"Yes."

Raphael touched Sara's curls. She had her hair down to her shoulders. Panic filled her as he touched her hair.

"There is a lot of work to be done on your hair."

Sara frowned and slapped his hand away. "What is wrong with my hair?" She snapped. "Do you brush it?"

"I am a black woman! Of course, my hair is different from Arabic women. The way I maintain it is different too!" *What a poor defensive line,* Sara thought.

"Race has nothing to do with it," Raphael said calmly. "It's just you who does not maintain it well."

Sara rolled her eyes. "Good night, Raphael," she said. She turned on her heel and stalked to the exit.

Chapter Five

Raphael was sitting in his office listening to Malik. He had finally addressed the press in regards to pictures of Raphael and Sara. Malik had told them that Raphael and Sara were engaged. However, the press was not buying it. They had more questions; why was it only being announced now? Why didn't Raphael address the issue himself?

"I do not want to hold a press conference to talk about Sara and me," Raphael said.

"You will not have to, but you will have to announce your engagement," said Malik.

Raphael leaned back in his chair.

"I will."

"You and Miss Pierce have to debut as a couple and the best time to do that will be this weekend at the Alexandria horse race."

Raphael always attended the annual Alexandria horse race. He loved horses. He even had a ranch at his home, and went riding when he had time. The idea of taking Sara to the race with him made sense. However, he had not introduced her to his family yet. It was only his Aunt Mariam that had seen her, and knew about her.

Raphael knew that he was going to have a hand in what she was going to wear. He found himself remembering her from the previous night. She had just wandered into his chambers, dressed in unflattering nightwear and messy hair. He had touched her hair to prove a point, but he found himself liking how it felt. It was softer that it looked.

"So how is it living with her?" Malik asked.

"She is not as easy to control as I hoped her to be."
Raphael liked to be in control of everything. Things
had to go his way. Unfortunately, it was not the case
with Sara. When he proposed the contract to her, she
had not jumped at the opportunity. Most women
wanted to be with him and would do anything to be
with him.

"She is a feisty one. I could not get her to sign the
NDA when I first met her."

"She might need to be tamed."

Malik laughed because he knew Raphael would do it.
He was always true to his words.

* *

"Raphael! What are you doing? Get out!" Sara
screamed out. She clutched onto the white towel that
was wrapped around her wet body.

"It's nothing I have not seen before." Raphael
continued walking into her bedroom, despite her
telling him to get out. He was holding an outfit and a
pair of shoes.

"Well, you haven't seen mine!"

Raphael stopped walking and just glared at her from
head to toe. His gaze lingered a little bit too long on
her legs. They were toned and a nice hazelnut color.

"Stop looking!" Sara shouted. Raphael put the clothes
and shoes on the bed.

"Like I said, it's nothing I have not seen before."

"What are those clothes for?"

"That is what you will wear today."

They were going to the Alexandria horse race. It was
Raphael's first time ever going there with a woman.
No doubt, the press was going to make a big deal out

of it. Of course, he was going to pick out her outfit. He could not afford to have anything go wrong.

"Are you kidding me right now?" Sara placed her hands on her hips.

"I do not kid."

"You must be if you think that I will wear that." Sara looked at the outfit. "It's not my style."

"Must we have this conversation again?" Raphael asked her.

"What conversation?"

"The one where I tell you that a sheikh's wife must dress and conduct herself in a certain way."

Sara growled. She really did not want to wear the outfit. She hated being controlled. No one had ever controlled her. Unfortunately, her father had passed away years ago. So she did not have male figures in her life telling her what to do.

"Okay, can you just leave so that I can change?" The fact that she was still in her towel and he was just standing before her like it was normal was just strange. He turned on his heel and left the room.

Sara wore the outfit that Raphael had picked out for her. A white satin boat neck dress hugged her chest and then flared from her mid-section to her calves. She pinned up her hair and arranged the white saucer fascinator at the front. She wore the low white heels he had picked for her. It was an outfit she would have never picked out for herself.

She finally emerged from her room. Raphael was waiting for her outside her room. He was already dressed in a navy blue suit and a crisp white shirt. "You aren't wearing your ring," Raphael pointed out to Sara.

"Oh yeah." She ran back into her room to get it. She was not used to wearing an engagement ring. She picked it up from the nightstand and slipped it on. She rushed back out of her room.

Raphael and Sara headed out of the palace together. There was a black Rolls Royce Phantom parked outside. The driver opened the door for them. Raphael allowed Sara to get in first. She got in and sat on the right side. The seats were made of cream colored leather. There was a small flat screen TV hanging from the ceiling.

The inside of the car was very nice. Sara did not have car, nor could she drive. She had never been inside such a beautiful car. Suddenly her phone vibrated. She pulled it out of her purse. It was a text message from her mother. "*Hello darling. It still weird to be here without you but we are fine. We miss you and hope your new job is going well. Treatment is going okay, so do not worry too much about me. Love you.*"

Sara felt bad that she still had not told her that she was not working but she was getting married. Her mother would probably try to stop her if she knew. She would feel guilty that Sara was doing it for her.

Sara missed her little sisters. They were still so young and with their mom being sick, they had no one. Sara had been like a second mother to them. She took them to school, the movies, checked their homework and played with them. It was hard not being able to see them.

"Are you alright?" Raphael asked Sara, as if he were actually concerned for her.

"Just a message from my mother," Sara replied as she slipped the phone back into her purse.

"How is treatment?"

"She says that it is going well."

"You do not believe her."

"No, I do not. She always hides things from me so that I do not worry."

"Should you need to go see her, tell me and I will have my pilot fly you over."

Sara was surprised by Raphael's generosity. He had always been off with her. They barely had a personal conversation. "Thank you," Sara said to him. She was going to take him up on that offer because she needed to see her mother. She was worried about her. Raphael did not respond to her.

Moments later, they arrived at the racecourse. Sara took a deep breath before she got out of the car. Raphael held his hand out to her. She took it and allowed him to help her out.

"Are you ready?" Raphael asked Sara.

"As I can be."

"There will be a lot of people, so much press-"

"I remember everything Mariam taught me this week." Sara and Mariam had been working together for the whole week. Sara had tried to get out of it but failed. The second day of Sara's so-called training with Mariam, Mariam had clothes delivered for Sara. The clothes that she had brought from America had been deemed unsuitable.

"Good," Raphael said and started walking.

"Raphael!" Sara called out.

"What?" He stopped and looked at her.

"We are coming as an engaged couple."

"So?"

"We should look the part."

Raphael looked confused. Sara could tell he knew nothing about women and romance. She rolled her eyes and linked her arms into his.

"What are you doing?" he asked her.

"Looking the part."

As they started walking, paparazzi approached them, taking photographs and calling them. "Sheikh! Sheikh!" they called.

"Is that your fiancé? What's her name?" they asked.

Sara did not know if they were meant to stop and talk to them. She just kept her head down and hung onto Raphael. It was all too much for her.

Chapter Six

Sara and Raphael sat in one of the executive boxes. Fortunately, the press was not allowed up there but there were other sheikhs in the box. Sara had not anticipated the company. They all stared at Raphael and Sara as they walked in.

"Sheikh Tadros," one of the sheikhs greeted him. Raphael shook his hand.

"I trust that your family is well," Raphael replied.

"They are well. Thank you for your concern."

"Sheikh Tadros junior," one of the other sheikhs said as he approached Raphael. The older man was dressed in a charcoal grey suit. He had at least fifteen years on Raphael. It made Sara actually wonder how old Raphael was. She had never asked him. She was twenty-four years old. She assumed that he was at least thirty years old.

"Sheikh Hosny," Raphael replied. His tone was not friendly. The two men shook hands. Sheikh Hosny turned his attention to Sara.

"I hear you are engaged," he said. Sara was not sure what to say or do. So she just smiled at the sheikh instead.

"Yes. We are engaged," said Raphael. Sara moved closer to him. That was the perfect moment for him to wrap his arm around her or something. However, he seemed to be clueless about women.

"We only just found out you were even seeing someone." Sheikh Hosny looked at Sara. "I am Sheikh Hosny and I work with your fiancé."

"I am Sara. Nice to meet you," Sara replied. Raphael should have been the one to introduce her.

"The pleasure is all mine."

Sara smiled. "I hope to see you at the wedding."

"I would not miss it for the world."

"The race is starting. We shall take our seats." Raphael went to sit down and Sara followed him and sat next to him. He leaned closer to Sara.

"What are you doing?"

He whispered in her ear, "You hope to see him at the wedding?"

"What else was I supposed to say?"

"Nothing."

"It was awkward. Blame yourself for not knowing how to even pretend as if you are in love. Hold me or something."

"I bet you would like that."

At that moment, it was very tempting. Raphael smelled nice. His body was very tempting. She pushed him away. She started giggling when she saw one of the sheikhs looking at them. She looked awkwardly at the tracks. The race was just starting.

"Which horse do we support?" Sara asked Raphael.

"Number eight."

"Okay." Sara did not know what to expect. She had never been to race before. A waitress came and asked them if they wanted anything to eat or drink. "What's good here?" Sara asked Raphael. He looked at her with a blank facial expression. Sara grinned at him.

The waitress recited the menu to them. "I'll try the aloe vera drink please," Sara said with a smile.

"Yes ma'am." The waitress left. Raphael had not said he wanted anything.

"Ma'am." Sara repeated with a frown.

"What is wrong now?" Raphael asked.

"I am too young to be called ma'am."

"She was being polite."

"But ma'am makes it sound like I am a fifty year old woman. Speaking of age, how old are you?"

Raphael raised his eyebrows. "You are curious."

"Yes, I am curious."

"Too bad, I am not going to tell you."

"Why not? It's not like you do not already know everything about me," Sara complained.

Raphael raised his eyebrows.

"I do not know everything about you."

"I meant that you did a background check on me. So you must know my age."

"I do."

"Then tell me yours."

Raphael smiled and looked away. Before Sara could protest, the waitress came with her drink. "Thank you," Sara said to her. She took a sip of the drink. "Oh, it tastes nice." Raphael just shook his head.

The races began. Sara was not sure how she was to act in this situation. She tried to sit like how Mariam taught her, but it was painful and exhausting. She kept fidgeting, trying to find a more comfortable position.

"What is wrong with you?" Raphael asked Sara quietly.

"Nothing." She shifted again, and Raphael held her thigh to stop her from moving. Sara's eyes flew open. The touch was so sudden and unexpected. She wanted to slap his hand away, but she could not. There were too many eyes on them.

The next race began. After watching the first race, Sara thought that racing was not so bad. She became more invested because the number eight horse was now racing. "Come on," she cheered.

Sara started getting excited. Worked up. The horse they were rooting for was in second place. "Come on," she cheered again. Raphael just stared at her. "Yes!" she shouted and threw her arms in the air when the horse won.

"Sara put your hands down," Raphael said to her. Sara awkwardly put her hands down. The other sheikhs had been cheering silently. One of the other sheikhs started laughing.

"She is spirited," he said to Raphael.

"Tell me about it," Raphael said with a forced smile.

"We need more spirited young ladies like that," the other sheikh said and laughed.

***

"When were you planning on telling me?"

Raphael heard a very familiar voice speak. He looked up from his desk and found his beautiful mother standing before him. He rose from his desk immediately. "Mother," he said as he walked around the desk and went to greet her. He kissed her on both cheeks.

"What brings you by?"

"I came to meet my future daughter-in-law," she replied. Raphael cleared his throat.

"Yes, I was going to tell you about that."

"When exactly?"

"Soon." Raphael had not actually decided on when he was going to tell his mother. She had been waiting for him to get married. She had been nagging him for years.

"Soon? I cannot believe you. Raphael I had to find out from the tabloids."

"I know. The press photographed us before we got the opportunity to tell the world." Raphael gestured for her to have a seat at his sofa. The two of them sat down.

"That is no excuse. You should have brought her to me before you even proposed to her. I need to know what kind of woman she is and what kind of family she came from."

Before Raphael could answer her, Sara rushed into the office. "Raphael! I need to ask--"Sara said as she walked into Raphael's office. She immediately stopped talking when she saw that he had company. Raphael and his both mother looked at her.

"Sorry, I will come back later," Sara said. She was barefoot and wearing shorts and a t-shirt.

"No, stay," said Raphael's mother. She eyed Sara from head to toe. "You must be my son's fiancé."

Sara's eyes flew open. "You are Raphael's mother." Sara was feeling rather awkward. Of all times to meet her, it had to be when she had rushed out of her room barefoot. Of course, something like that would happen to Sara.

"Yes dear, please join us."

"You can talk with her properly on another occasion," said Raphael. He looked a little annoyed. No doubt, it was because the way Sara was dressed.

"No, I especially came here today to see her." She gestured for Sara to join them at the sofas. Sara sat on the sofa facing Raphael and his mother.

"My name is Sara. Nice to meet you." Sara bowed her head and smiled.

"Where did you and my son meet?"

Oh no! Sara felt a little bit panic inside of her. She and Raphael had not discussed the fine details. They did not have a story of when they first met, or how he proposed to her.

"We can talk about that later," said Raphael.

"I want to know, because this relationship is very sudden to me," said Mrs. Tadros.

"We met in Dallas," said Sara.

"Is that where you are from?"

"Yes."

"And what was it that attracted you to my son?"

Nothing at all! He's arrogant and controlling, Sara really wanted to say but for obvious reasons, she could not. "He is a responsible and interesting man."

Mrs. Tadros started laughing.

"Interesting?" she asked.

"Yes, he is different from other men. He's candid, generous, and articulate. He is his own man."

"So, were you two that much in love that you have decided to move in together before the wedding?"

"Once we were photographed together, I knew that Sheikh Hosny would try to get a hold of her and try to use this story to his advantage. So it was only natural that I moved her into my home earlier than the wedding," said Raphael.

She remembered Sheikh Hosny. He had been almost nice to her, but she felt that there was something off. Even Raphael was not pleased when Sara said that she hoped to see him at the wedding. However, after hearing him say that he would try to approach Sara and use the story to his advantage, it made Sara

171

realize that there was something deeper between the sheikh and Raphael.

"I know that man is quite cunning," said Mrs. Tadros. "But living together before marriage?"

"We have not shared a bed together," said Sara. Mrs. Tadros and her son both raised their eyebrows at her.

"I see," said Mrs. Tadros.

"Sara is quite candid, too."

Sara wondered if she had said anything inappropriate. She had only clarified what his mother was worried about.

Mrs. Tadros smiled. "She is. Well, the two of you need to come for dinner at my house. You need to introduce her to your father," she said.

"We will do that."

"And then we can discuss the wedding. Make time tomorrow."

"Tomorrow?"

"It was not a request, my dear."

"Yes, mother."

Chapter 7

Sara and Raphael sat in the back of the Rolls Royce Phantom, heading to meet with Raphael's parents. Raphael was still scolding her because of what she had worn the day before. "Barefoot, Sara! Seriously, you could not wear shoes," he said.

"Well, we were at home and indoors. So, of course I was barefoot. How would I have known that your mother was coming over?"

"This is why I sent Mariam to you."

"Well, what's done is done, and I do not regret it. I was being comfortable at home."

Raphael shook his head. "What were you even doing in my chambers?" he asked her.

"I needed to speak to you."

"And it could not wait?"

"No, it could not!" Sara fingered a small curly lock of hair just by the temple of her head. She had her hair in a high bun.

"What did you need to speak to me about?"

"This, everything!" Sara was feeling frustrated and worried.

"You are not thinking about backing out now, are you?"

"Of course not. It's just that I need to see my mother, see how she's coping with treatment. But the issue is that I don't know how to tell her about all of this." Sara could not just get married and not tell her mother. Raphael's family would also wonder why her family never attended the wedding.

"You can go see her tomorrow and invite her to the wedding."Sara stared at him with a blank stare.

"What? Did you not hear what I just said? I do not know how to tell her."

"Remember, you signed a contract. You will just have to tell her that you found the man of your dreams and all that crap."

"Crap." Sara shook her head.

"Yes, all of this love and skipping heart beats is crap."

"So you do not believe in love? It explains why you are thirty-two years old and unwed."

Raphael looked at her with amusement on his face. "So you found out my age."

"That is not what we are talking about right now." She had Googled him after they had returned from the Alexandria horse racing.

"Then what are we talking about?"

The car came to a halt. "You are incredibly frustrating," she said. She looked out of the window and realized that they were parked up outside a grand residence.

"So are you going to see your mother tomorrow or not?" Raphael asked. Sara whipped her head in his direction and frowned. There was no compassion in his voice.

"Yes, I am."

"I will tell the pilot to be ready," he said. "You must tell your family about the engagement soon, because we are getting married two weeks from today."

"What?" Sara screamed out. He had told her from the beginning that they were going to wed quickly, but not that quick. They had not even discussed anything about the wedding since she got there. They barely spoken about anything.

"What are you so shocked about?"

The driver opened the door.

"Two weeks?"

Raphael got out of the car. Sara also got out. She was wearing a knee-length, white, boat neck dress. It had three-quarter lace sleeves with embroidery on them. She wore low beige heels with it. Raphael was wearing a white shirt and beige tailored pants.

"I assume you are going to hold my arm again," Raphael said to Sara.

"Yes." She linked her arm into his. "I swear you know nothing about women."

"I assure you I know plenty."

Sara laughed sarcastically. "Okay, then."

"Behave yourself when we are inside."

They walked down the stone pavement leading up to the mansion. Sara barely had time to enjoy her surroundings because she was too busy arguing with Raphael. "What do you mean behave yourself?" she asked him.

"I would have said remember what Mariam taught you but it seems that you have not learned anything."

"Talking to me like that is not going to make me obedient. It is only making me want to do the opposite."

Raphael looked at her as if she had gone mad. She was testing him. Before he could say anything to her, the maids opened the door for them.

"Welcome, Sheikh Raphael," the two maids said. They looked at Sara. "Welcome, Miss," they said. Sara smiled at them.

"Thank you," she replied.

Still holding onto his arm, Sara followed Raphael into the house. They walked down the hall and then into a large room, where some of Raphael's family members were. The ceilings were high. There were some intricate, colorful designs on the top part of the walls, and painting on the bottom half. Golden crystal chandeliers hung from the ceiling. There were low cream sofas against the walls decorated with different colored pillows.

"Raphael, you are here, at last," one woman said as she got up from the sofas. She was a little bit taller than Sara. She had long straight jet-black hair and nicely shaped dark eyebrows. Her honey colored skin glowed. She wore a coral sleeveless dress and flat shoes. "They are even holding hands," she pointed out.

Raphael released his arm from Sara's. He kissed the woman on both cheeks. "I trust that you have been well, Maria." Sara noticed that he said, "I trust that you have been well" to people, instead of asking how they were. He was a strange man.

"I'm fine," said Maria. She turned her attention to Sara. "You must be Sara," she said and went to kiss her on both cheeks.

"Hello," Sara said with a smile on her face. From the corner of her eye, she saw Mariam and Mrs. Tadros drinking tea. They put cups down and started walking towards Sara and Raphael.

"I am Maria, Raphael's cousin," she said. She looked no more than twenty-six years old.

"Nice to meet you."

"Sara, welcome dear," said Mrs. Tadros. She and Mariam both kissed Sara and Raphael on both cheeks.

Sara had not expected to see Mariam. Even though they saw each other every day during the last week, they were not close. Sara did not want all those etiquette lessons and what not. However, Mariam was strict on Sara and did not allow her to slack.

"Where is Father?" Raphael asked his mother.

"In the dining room with your brothers discussing business. We must go join them."

They all headed out of the room. As they were walking, Sara held Raphael's arm and whispered a question to him. "What's this room?" she asked.

"The drawing room," he said. Sara wondered about people who still had drawing rooms in this day and age.

The dining room was just as impressive as the drawing room. The floors were also made of white marble. The ceiling was also high. There were golden embroideries on the ceiling. There was a long table in the middle of the room. It was filled with different types of Arabic foods that made Sara's mouth water.

"Raphael," an older man said when he laid his eyes on Raphael.

"Father." Sara did not understand the rest. He started speaking in Arabic. There two other men in the room. Sara assumed that they were Raphael's brothers. They approached her.

"You must be our new sister-in-law," one of them said to Sara. "I am Jamal, Raphael's youngest brother."

"And I am Fady, the middle one," the other said, and smiled at Sara. They both were as tall as Raphael, but less muscular. However, they still had athletic bodies. They looked like Raphael.

177

"Nice to meet you both, I am Sara." She had introduced herself so many times that week, it was getting tiring. It was also awkward. It was crazy that in less than six months, she was not going to know those people.

"Come, let me look at you," Raphael's father said to Sara. He held her shoulders and studied her face. He too was tall, but just three inches shorter than his sons. "She is beautiful. I wonder why you kept her from us," he said to Raphael.

"The engagement was sudden," said Raphael. Mr. Tadros laughed.

"Well, you can tell us all about it over dinner." He gestured everyone to sit down.

As they ate, they took turns bombarding questions to Raphael and Sara. They were all curious about their relationship. He had never introduced anyone to them. He rarely spoke of his relationships, and yet here he was, engaged and ready to marry in the next week.

"Must you rush the wedding?" Mrs. Tadros asked. "Is she pregnant?"

"No, nothing like that," said Raphael.

"They are in love," said Maria. "Have you ever seen him holding anyone's hand?"

Jamal said, "Oh, they came in holding hands?"

"They did. And then there was that photo of them in Dallas. Flirting in public!"

Sara responded awkwardly. They were hardly flirting. It was crazy how that one misunderstanding had caused all of that.

"He hardly flirts," said Sara.

"What is it like being with Raphael?" Maria asked Sara.

"Maria," said Raphael.

"What? I am curious. We all thought that the only way you were ever going to marry was through an arranged marriage." Maria looked at Sara. "He never believed in love, you see."

Sara smiled. "No he did not. That was why his proposal was surprising. He said he could not live without me." After she said that, she watched Raphael's face change. She had done that purposely just to play with him.

"Sara," Raphael said.

"Really?" Maria was shocked. Sara smiled and nodded. She tried so hard not to laugh.

"Yes, that is why the wedding is so soon. He says that he cannot wait to make me his wife."

"Oh, my." Maria placed her hand on her chest and blushed. Raphael's brothers were laughing. He was just chewing angrily. Sara knew that they were going to argue on their way back home.

*

As soon as the driver shut the door, Raphael turned to face Sara. He could not believe what she had done during dinner. She had a slight smirk on her face as she spoke. He knew she was deliberately trying to annoy him because he did not believe in love. The even crazier thing was the fact that his family believed her, especially Maria.

"You must have lost your mind," Raphael said to Sara. "You dared to utter such lies in front my family."

Sara started laughing. "Your face was funny."

"This is no laughing matter." He could not believe that she found this funny. The worst thing is that he found her lips incredibly enticing. She had nice, soft and luscious looking lips. It was a shame that she could only use them to argue with him and laugh at inappropriate times.

"Why are you so annoyed by what I said?" Sara asked him, as if she had no clue.

"Because those were lies!" Raphael snapped. He told her to behave herself. Why was she so stubborn and talkative? Was it that hard to sit there quietly?

"This whole marriage is a lie," Sara whispered so that the driver would not hear. "So stop overreacting. We are so supposed to act all in love. Why is it so hard for you to play along when it benefits you?"

"Why must you be this stubborn?"

"Why are you this rigid?"

"You are frustrating!"

"So are you."

"Recant your attitude. I do not appreciate it." She spoke so freely towards him, it was not right. He was not used to being disrespected like that.

"I am reciprocating. I will treat you the way you treat me." Sara folded her arms over her chest and looked away. Just as he was about to say something, he caught a glimpse of her legs. She sat with her legs parted like a man, the way Mariam had advised against. Her dress sat on her thighs, revealing them slightly.

It reminded him of when he walked in on her with a towel wrapped her wet body. He could never get that image out of his head. The look of her legs enticed him. He leaned forward and pulled Sara's dress down. "What are you doing?" she asked and smacked his hand away.

"Covering your legs, because you do not conduct yourself like a lady," he snapped. He wanted to run his hand up her thighs instead but he controlled himself.

"There is no one here!"

"If you get used to conducting yourself in a certain manner in private, then it will become habit--"

Before he finished making his point, Sara cut him off. "Okay, Sheikh Raphael, I get it."

It was the first time she had called him sheikh. However, it was quite sarcastic. She really needed discipline.

Fortunately, they arrived back home. Raphael could no longer be in the same car as her. Part of him was angry with her and wanted to scold her for her behavior. However, the other part of him wanted to caress her lovely hazelnut colored legs and just rip her dress open.

Sara opened the car door for herself and got out of the car. She took her shoes off and walked towards the front door. Raphael shook his head. She was walking barefoot again.

"Are you serious right now?" he asked her.

"What now?"

"Put your shoes back on."

"No." Sara turned away from him and started walking. He quickly caught up with her and scooped her up into his arms. He did not want her to walk into the house like that. The maids would start talking. She was going to be the sheikh's wife. There were things she was not meant to be seen doing.

"Put me down!" Sara screamed. She hit him on the chest a few times but he did not release her.

"Either stay still or put your shoes back on."

"You have issues."

The security guards opened the door for them. As they walked into the house, the maids stopped and stared. Sara stopped fighting him. "This is better actually. Let the maids see you carrying me in your arms. It's quite romantic."

"I know what you are trying to do." Raphael walked up the stairs.

"What I am trying to do?"

"So now you want to play dumb."

Sara laughed. "You are an interesting man."

"And you are a peculiar woman." Raphael never argued with people. His word was final. However, he found himself going back and forth with Sara. He walked into her room with her and threw her on the bed. She screamed as she landed.

"What is the matter with you?!" she called out.

"You should have just worn your shoes."

Sara got on her knees and placed her hands on her hips. Raphael knew that she was not pleased about him throwing her onto the bed, but he didn't care. Just as she was about to say something, her phone vibrated.

"You are lucky," she said to him, and pulled her phone out of her purse.

"What would you have done?" he asked her. She did not scare him. He watched her face drop as she read the message on her phone. She sighed heavily.

"What is wrong with you now?" he asked her. Raphael was used to seeing full spirited, witty, sarcastic and stubborn. Right now, she looked a bit sad.

"Just a message from my little sisters."

"So, why aren't you happy?" Raphael approached Sara.

"Because they just said they miss me. It's not easy being away from them."

"How old are they?"

"Ten, but you already knew that." Sara looked at him with a blank facial expression. It seemed that she was not over the fact that he had done a background check on her.

Raphael cupped her chin.

"Is it possible for you to speak to me without getting angry about something?"

"Well, only if you stop making me angry."

"You will get to see them tomorrow, so don't be so sad."

Sara nodded. "Thank you for letting me use the jet." She looked at him with her brown eyes widened and screaming innocence. Her lips said something different. They looked so full and tempting.

Raphael moved closer to her. "It's fine."

"But why are you still holding my face?"

"I am holding your chin and not your face."

"Well, same difference. My chin is on my face."

"I think you just enjoy arguing with me."

"Don't be so conceited," she said. Raphael did not respond to her. He couldn't figure what it was about her that allowed himself to go back and forth with her. He never did so with anyone. He just gazed at her. Sara's skin was just so beautiful. He caressed her jaw with his thumb. Her skin was just as soft as he had anticipated. However, he had not anticipated it to be addictive. He wanted to keep touching her.

Her lip twitched, giving him the push he needed. He lowered his head and moved his face closer to hers. Sara maintained eye contact. Raphael moved closer and closer until their faces were an inch away from each other. Their noses touched. He parted his lips, and just as he was about to kiss her, her phone started ringing.

They both moved back and looked at each other in shock, as if they had just been caught. Sara cleared her throat and looked at her phone. "My sisters again."

"Talk to them." Raphael said. He turned on his heel and stalked to the exit.

Chapter 8

Sara was sitting in Raphael's private jet, almost in Dallas. It was crazy to her how she had just gotten on a private jet, just like that. Months ago, she would have struggled with bus fare for the week. She glanced at her engagement ring and suddenly felt butterflies in her stomach. She and Raphael had almost kissed the night before.

This man that she was always arguing with, and just didn't agree with on anything, was about to kiss her and she was going to let him. Her heart had started racing. His stroking of her jaw had not helped. She was disappointed that she had not gotten the opportunity to taste his gorgeous lips. She was a little annoyed that her phone rang.

"Miss, please buckle your seatbelt. We are about to land," the flight attendant said to her. Sara snapped out of her thoughts and nodded.

When she arrived at the airport, there was a car waiting for her. She was surprised that Raphael had even bothered to arrange that for her. She hopped into the back seat and thanked the driver. He shut the door behind her, and then got into the driver's seat.

She arrived home moments later. It was just after 4 pm, so she knew that everyone would be home. She fished the keys out of her bag and unlocked the door.

"Sara!" Sara's twin sisters shouted and ran into her arms.

"Hi," Sara said and held them tightly. She kissed both of them on their foreheads. "I missed the two of you."

"We missed you, too."

Sara's mother walked out of the kitchen. Sara had never been so happy to see her mother. She immediately rushed into her arms and held her tightly. "I missed your scent," she said.

Her mother laughed.

"What an interesting surprise." She pulled Sara out of her arms and held her by her shoulders. "Why did you come back so soon? Were things not going well?"

"Things are fine. I just missed you guys." Her little sisters were standing at her sides.

"Liar, you were worried about me. As I told you in the message, things are fine. Treatment is going well. Treatment is going very well."

Sara studied her mother from head to toe. She then looked at her sisters. "Has Mom been okay?" she asked them.

"Yes," the twins chorused.

"Don't you believe your mother?"

"I know you don't want me to worry, so you conceal things from me."

Sara's mother smiled and rubbed her arms. The two of them headed to the kitchen and left the twins to watch their cartoons. Sara smiled when she walked into their tiny kitchen, filled with the smell of her mother's cooking. She had missed it.

"What has been happening in Egypt?" her mother asked, as she chopped the onions.

"It's not home," Sara replied. Her mother stopped chopping and looked at Sara.

"What is really going on?"

"What do you mean?"

"All of a sudden there is money for my treatment and you have a job in Egypt. Did you meet someone?" her mother asked. Sara raised her eyebrows. She was not sure what to say, she could not keep anything from her mother.

Sara did not know how to start. She fished the ring out of her bag and handed it to her mother. She took it and looked at the ring. Her eyes flew open. "Sara." Her mother just trailed off. She was in shock. She looked at Sara. "An engagement ring? Start talking because I didn't see anyone coming here to ask for your hand in marriage."

"It just kind of happened."

"Just happened? And this guy can afford to buy such a pricey ring."

"He's doing okay." Talk about downplaying. Raphael owned a mansion, a jet and was going to be the CEO of the biggest oil company in the Middle East. He was more than okay.

"Okay?" Sara's mother laughed. "This ring is worth hundreds of thousands of dollars. He is more than okay."

Sara itched the back of head awkwardly. "Please don't freak out."

Her mother switched the stove off and crossed her arms over her chest. She gave Sara her full attention, which made Sara more nervous.

Sara decided to tell her mother everything, even though she had told herself she shouldn't. She knew that her mother would be against it. She also could not tell her mother about it because she had signed a non-disclosure agreement. As she told her mother the story, her mother's face changed. It was clear that she was shocked.

"Sara." Her mother stopped talking and just stood there with her hand on her chest. "You." She just could not find the words to say.

"I know it is reckless and you prob-"

"Want to kill you? Yes I do. What the hell are you thinking?" Her mother hit her arm.

"Ouch!" Sara cried out. Her mum tried to hit her again but she quickly dodged and ran to the other side of the kitchen, not that it was a big kitchen, anyway.

"Sara this is by far the craziest and most irresponsible thing you have ever done!"

Sara was not surprised that her mother was just ready to kill her. The situation was crazy, irrational and impulsive.

However, the only thing she was thinking about at the time was her mother's health. Nothing else mattered.

"I know, Mom, but I already signed the contract." Sara was not making it any better. She was not arguing her case properly nor was she convincing her mother that she had not made a good decision.

"A contract marriage? Are you crazy? Sara this is your life. You cannot just throw away like that."

"I am not throwing it away, it's temporary."

Her mother narrowed her gaze at her. "So by the age of twenty-five, you are going to be a divorcee. That's not throwing your life away." The level of sarcasm in the last sentence was very high. Sara knew she definitely had it from her.

"I know, but I won't regret it."

"Because you are doing it for us? For me?"

"For myself."

"You have never been an opportunist or materialistic. So it's not for yourself."

"I want to do this because it benefits all of you. I would never be okay if I knew that I didn't do everything in my power to look after you, the twins and myself."

Her mother shook her head. "I am the mother; I look after you and not the other way around." She sounded like she was blaming herself and that was not what Sara wanted.

"Life happens and we all have to take responsibilities. It's okay, Mom. I am okay with this. Please be okay with it and come to the wedding." Sara decided to throw the wedding invitation in there. It was better to get everything out all at once.

"Really, Sara?" Her mother shook her head.

"Well, his family would wonder where you are, and it is my first wedding."

"First wedding." She sighed deeply. Sara moved closer to her and tugged at her arm.

"I need you through this. I know I should have told you sooner but I knew you would not like the idea."

"Damn right, I don't like it."

Sara wrapped her arms around her mother. "So you'll come?"

"I need to see this man and make sure that he will looking after you. However, I am finding it difficult that you moved out to Egypt without telling me and you were living with him." Her mother pushed Sara away and stared at her with her eyebrows raised.

"I did not sleep with him, I swear!"

After her mother had calmed down, Sara was able to talk to her and just catch her up on everything. Her mother agreed to come to the wedding and play along, but she was not happy about it. Sara was happy to have dinner with her family. It was not made by some accomplished chef or served by some maids, but it was better. She caught up with her sisters on what had been going on since she left.

Sara slept in her single bed that she had owned for as long as she could remember. As she tried falling asleep, thoughts of Raphael surfaced in her head. It was odd not seeing him. She didn't miss him but it felt like there was something missing. She was used to seeing him every day; arguing with him and bumping heads on every topic at hand. Sara just shook her head. She was in her home with her family; there was no reason to be thinking about Raphael.

*

Raphael sat in a meeting with all the other sheikhs. It was his father's last meeting as the CEO of Salam Oils & Gasses. His father had felt that he had been in office for long enough and he wanted to leave it to Raphael so that he could focus on other business ventures. Some of the sheikhs were happy to let Raphael be the next CEO, but Sheikh Hosny and his followers were not pleased.

Sheikh Hosny wanted to take over the company. He wanted that seat for himself. However, it was not so easy, when he did not have the most shares in the company. Raphael sat there listening to him listing reasons as to why Raphael was not ready to lead the company. He slowly started drifting off and thinking about Sara.

The last time he had seen her, they had almost kissed. Damn her phone that had to ring when he was about to kiss her. Raphael groaned. She was not appealing. She was not his type. She didn't look after her image and she was so stubborn. But why had he wanted to kiss her and why was he thinking about her?

"How is your bride to be?" Sheikh Hosny asked Raphael after the meeting.

"She is quite well."

"Please pass her my regards." Sheikh Hosny moved closer to Raphael and whispered in his ear. "There is something off about her and I will find it."

"What are you talking about?"

"I do not believe that you could just pull a fiancé out of your hat, just like that." Sheikh Hosny tapped Raphael's shoulder and left.

Raphael grunted. That man was really getting on his last nerve. He fought Raphael at every turn. It was exhausting. It slightly bothered him that Hosny questioned Raphael's engagement, but he was not surprised. It made him feel better that his family was already planning the wedding. His mother and Maria were very eager to plan it. He did not have to worry about the wedding.

Sara was in Raphael's chambers when he arrived home. "You're back."

Sara turned around to look at him. Strangely, her hair looked very thick and bouncy. He wanted to touch it.

"I am. I had just come over to speak to you." Sara explained herself for being in his chambers. He was not even bothered as to why she was there.

"How is your family?"

"They're fine. Thanks for lending me the jet."

He dismissed her gratitude with his hand. "Were you able to tell them about the wedding?"

Sara nodded. "I did. It was not easy." She laughed nervously.

"Why not?"

"Well because my mother has never met you nor had she heard anything about you. So she was shocked and not too pleased about it."

Raphael gave her half a smile and nodded. Even his mother was shocked about the engagement.

Sara gasped. "It's a miracle."

"What is a miracle?" he asked her.

"You smiled."

Raphael narrowed his gaze at her and loosened his tie. She had never smiled at him either, he thought to himself. It was going to be a crazy six months for the two of them. He also noticed that Sara was happier. It seemed as though going to visit her mother had lifted her spirits.

"So I was at the airport when some random guy stopped me," Sara said as she sat down on the sofa.

"Okay?" Raphael was confused as to why she was telling him.

"Well, listen first." Sara shook her head. "Anyway, this guy, this man, stopped and asked me about our relationship."

"He asked about us?" Raphael went to sit on the sofa in front of her. Sara nodded. "What did he ask?"

"All kinds of questions, about where we met, how long we have been dating, when we got engaged and just a lot of questions about us."

"What did he look like?"

"He was in smart wear. He clearly was not paparazzi but he was incredibly nosey. I didn't say anything to him. I told him that I was not going to divulge my personal matters to a stranger." Sara sighed.

"I assume that Sheikh Hosny had something to do with this."

"What is the big deal with you and that man?"

"He worked with my father for many years. Although he presented a loyal front, he was waiting to take my father's place. When my father announced that he wanted to retire and let me take over, he was not pleased."

"So he is trying to sabotage you?"

"Exactly."

"So that's why you approached me first in Dallas."

"Yes."

"How would he use me against you? I could easily refuse to talk."

"I did not know you. I could not take that chance. There are people that can be offered money and will do or say whatever needs to be said."

"True enough, but is marrying me the answer?"

Raphael grunted. He understood how it would not make sense to other people. He could easily have paid for her silence, but it still meant Sheikh Hosny could find her and still use her. He could not afford to leave any loose ends.

Even if Sara did not take Hosny up, that photo would be the start of rumors regarding his private life. Hosny would try to find his past lovers and get them to lie or find something about Raphael that he could use against him. Even if he made a statement about the photograph, it would look like he was trying to hide something.

"Yes, it is," Raphael finally replied. "Speaking of which, my family has been planning the wedding. This week you will have to get measured for the wedding dress and go pick out cakes."

Sara raised her eyebrows. She was not all that excited. "Can I just show up at the wedding?"

"Aren't you interesting in planning the wedding also? I hear women love these things."

"I don't," she replied. Raphael raised his eyebrows. "I know that the average girl starts planning her wedding from the age of six or something, but that is not me. You need the perfect man, not the perfect wedding."

"I honestly thought you would be into all that." Given the fact that love mattered to her, Raphael had assumed that she would also love to plan her perfect wedding. It showed to him that he did not know much about her, about the woman he was going to marry.

"I would not mind just a small wedding."

"Neither would I." Raphael smiled. Sara giggled.

"Jeez, first time we agreed on something."

"It is because you are so stubborn."

"I believe that you are equally stubborn." She said it with so much sass. "Let's go have dinner." She was looking at the gold plated watch hung up on the wall.

"You are hungry?"

Sara nodded. "I am starving and I am tired." Raphael nodded and rose from his sofa. Sara remained seated. Instead, she stretched her arms out for Raphael to help her up to her feet. He just looked at her with a blank facial expression.

"What is happening with you?" he asked, as if he did not know what she wanted. Sara burst out laughing.

"Aren't you going to help me up?" she asked.

"Why?"

"Oh my, this is why I say that you know nothing about women" Sara helped herself up.

Raphael grinned.

"One day, you will come to eat your words."

"Challenge accepted." She walked out of his chambers. He followed her.

**

It was two days before the wedding and Sara was feeling stressed. There had been so much to do in the last week. Raphael's mother and aunt were taking her to different places and just preparing for the wedding. She had wanted to stay out of the planning, but Mariam would not allow it. In the midst of all of that chaos, Mariam still taught Sara how to speak Arabic, how to cook some Arabic dishes, and about their culture.

Sara was fed up. She could not wait until after the wedding. She was sitting with Mariam, Mrs. Tadros and Maria. They were going over the seating arrangements, flowers to be used at the wedding and other finishing touches. Sara said she needed to go to the bathroom, but went to Raphael's chambers instead.

"What are you doing here?" Raphael asked Sara when she rushed in his office and shut the door. She was grateful that he was working from home that day.

"I can't take it anymore, Raphael."

"It cannot be that bad."

"It is that bad." Sara ran her hand through her hair. "They are picking out flowers. I swear they are all the same."

Raphael laughed. "That is what I always say, but somehow my mother can hold five flowers that look the same, and still divide them into sub categories." He went to the cabinet to retrieve a file.

"It's ridiculous. It was the same thing, the shades of beige." Sara threw herself on the sofa. "I can't wait to see my mother, though."

"That will be interesting." Raphael sat on the arm of the sofa and just looked at Sara lying on her back and facing upwards.

"Prepare yourself. She will ask you a thousand questions."

"I can handle her."

Sara sat up and looked at him. He had no idea what he was up against. "Do not take her lightly."

"I am sure if I can handle you, then I can handle your mother."

Sara raised her eyebrows and burst out laughing. "You can handle? No, you cannot." She held his shoulders and looked at him.

"There is nothing you have done or said that I could not handle."

Sara smiled. "I can see you having a hard time when I refuse to do something. You hate it when you lose control."

Raphael raised an eyebrow. "So you know when you are giving me a hard time and yet you continue."

Sara scratched the back of her head awkwardly. "It's not intentional. I just don't agree with you."

Raphael grunted. Sara was still holding onto his shoulders. He wrapped his arm around her waist and pulled her closer to him. He pressed a small kiss against her lips. The sudden touch of his lips against hers was unexpected. Sara had not anticipated a kiss. His lips were soft. He kissed her softly and gently. Sara kissed him back and wrapped one arm around his neck.

Sara's chest was pressed against Raphael's chest. She could feel the hardness of it. She held onto his biceps, which were equally hard. The feeling of his hard body and softness of his lips aroused her. She felt her whole body quickly igniting and responding to every stroke of his tongue in her mouth.

Chapter 9

Suddenly, Sara and Raphael heard the door open. They both stopped kissing and turned to look at the door. Mrs. Tadros was standing at the door with a smile on her face. "So this is where you disappeared to."

Sara quickly pulled back from Raphael and got off the sofa.

"I came to speak to him about something," Sara said. She could not believe that she and Raphael had just kissed. She was a little annoyed that they been disturbed.

"No need to give me an excuse. After all, it is your fiancé."

Raphael cleared his throat and walked back to his desk. "You may take her back." Sara whipped her head in his direction. She stared at him wide eyed. She had come to him to escape from his family. Now he was sending her back.

"Thank you, son," said Mrs. Tadros. "You will have all the time you need together after the wedding."

"Okay, I am coming," said Sara. She did not want to continue with this conversation. It would probably lead to honeymoon talk or grandchildren.

Sara's mother and sisters arrived later that night. Raphael had sent the jet to fly them to Egypt. Sara ran into the living room and saw her family there. She quickly rushed to hug them. "I am so glad you are here."

"Sara, we flew in a private jet," said Elizabeth; one of her sisters.

"Did you like it?"

"We did," both sisters chorused. Their mother was gaping at the living room.

"This is crazy, Sara. You mean to tell me that this fiancé of yours owns all of this? Including the jet?" Mrs. Pierce asked her daughter.

"Yes." Sara nodded. Raphael came down the stairs dressed in grey trousers and a crisp white shirt.

"Mrs. Pierce, you made it," he said as he approached her. "I am Raphael, Sara's fiancé." He kissed her on both cheeks. "I trust that you traveled well?"

There was that "*I trust...*" Line again. Sara tried not to laugh. It was so odd how he always said it and never actually asked.

"We had a comfortable flight, thank you," said Sara's mother. "It is funny how you introduce yourself as my daughter's fiancé but you never came to officially ask me for her hand in marriage."

Sara's eyes flew open. She had not expected her mother to get on Raphael's case immediately.

"I fully apologize for not doing that, Mrs. Pierce. Sara and I rushed into this, and it did not give us enough time to do things the right away."

Sara frowned. Why was he bringing her into this?

"That is no excuse. I need to know the man to whom I am going to be handing my daughter."

"I promise you that I am the man for her."

Sara looked at Raphael. He was what?

"Are you now?"

"Yes, Mrs. Pierce. Would you like to have a seat?"

"Yes, because this will be a lengthy discussion."

"Hello." Raphael greeted Sara's little sisters.

"Hi," they both said and just stared at him. Sara asked one of the maids to take her sisters to her room. The three of them sat down to talk. Sara and Raphael were sitting on the same sofa, facing Mrs. Pierce.

"So what are the concerns you wish for me to address?" Raphael asked her mother.

"This is not a business meeting. I am not going to just raise issues and you address them. You are going to marry my daughter in two days. I do not like it but I can't stop it. So help me understand why the wedding is being rushed and why you never met me beforehand."

Sara knew her mother wanted to see what Raphael was made of. She knew that it was a fake marriage and yet she questioned him. Sara sat back in her chair and watched everything unfold. She was not getting involved.

"I know I did not go about things the way you would want, and unfortunately, I cannot change it. However, I can promise you that I will not make Sara unhappy. She will be looked after emotionally, mentally and spiritually."

Sara looked at Raphael. Had Malik written him a script or something?"Your daughter is one of a kind. She's beautiful inside and out. She needs a man who can handle her sass and stubbornness, and a man who is not afraid to love her and provide for her."

Sara could not take it. She really wanted to laugh. This man was bullshitting. He did not even believe in love.

"I hope your words are true because if not, you will have to deal with me," said Mrs. Pierce.

"I am not only marrying Sara. I am also marrying you and your other daughters. I will also look after all of you and do my best to be the son-in-law you want. I hope you can give me a chance to show you that I am worth it."

Sara sat up and held onto Raphael's arm. "Who told you what to say?"

Raphael laughed and kissed her on the cheek.

"Not now, *habibti*," he said to her. "Excuse her. Your daughter always wants to drag me away for some quality time," he said to her mother.

Mrs. Pierce raised her eyebrows and looked at her daughter.

That night, at dinner, Raphael's family and Sara's were introduced to each other. They sat in the other dining room that Raphael used when entertaining guests. This one was bigger and more extravagant. A long table sat in the middle of the room with a crystal chandelier hanging from the ceiling above it. The chairs were cream with golden embroidery on them, and with golden legs and armrests. Expensive China plates were used to serve the different extravagant traditional Arabic dishes.

For the first half of the dinner, Mrs. Pierce and Mrs. Tadros were talking about how they should have met sooner. They were not happy that the first time they were meeting was only two days before the wedding. Thankfully, they seemed to be getting along. Sara had been worried about it because they were from two different backgrounds.

What was even more surprising was the fact that Mariam and Mrs. Pierce were getting along. They were on the same page in regards to teaching Sara to be more ladylike and learn about their culture. Sara looked at Raphael who was enjoying it and agreeing.

Well, of course he would have been, since it was his idea in the first place.

"Sara is fine the way she is. I think it's exactly what Raphael needs," said Maria.

"Thank you, at least someone is on my side," said Sara.

"What is it that I need?" Raphael asked.

"You need a strong woman who isn't afraid to challenge you and tame you."

Mariam and Mrs. Pierce started laughing.

"Tame him? As if that is possible," said Mariam.

"Haven't you noticed that he has already started changing?"

"He is?"

"I am?" Raphael asked.

"Who could not change with such a beautiful woman at his side?" Raphael's father asked.

"He has never been seen with any woman in public. He took her to the horse race, he never usually takes women, and they're always holding hands. He's so sweet with her," said Maria.

Sara wondered what Maria had been smoking because Raphael had not been sweet with her, except when he let her use the jet to go see her mother.

"Raphael is in love," Jamal joked. Sara felt her stomach knot up. She couldn't understand why she was getting nervous and shy.

"Well, he better have his last look now, because he will not see her until the wedding day," said Mariam.

Sara felt even more nervous. She looked at Raphael who was already looking at her with a dark gaze. Her heart started pounding faster. It made Sara even more nervous knowing she had no idea what he was thinking.

The day of the wedding finally arrived. Sara just wanted to get the day over and done with. She had already been up for hours. Mariam had brought over a glam squad for Sara. They had soaked her in a milk and honey bath for what felt like eternity, then applied natural oils to her skin and hair.

It took them three hours just to do Sara's hair. It needed washing, blow drying, straightening and curling. Her hair parted at the side and they styled into a vintage up do. Then there was the makeup application. Sara had to get her eyebrows threaded and shaped. The make-up artist applied a natural look for Sara.

Sara wore silver earrings. They were circular and made of lots of tiny diamonds in a circular pattern. She wore a silver diamond necklace matching the earrings and bracelet. Her boob tube wedding dress hugged her torso and then flared from the waist to her ankles. It had silver embroidery on the sides. Her long white veil was the last thing she wore.

"You look gorgeous," her mother said to her as she walked into the living room where she and the others had been waiting. She stared at her daughter with watery eyes. Mariam, Mrs. Tadros, Maria and the twins were looking at Sara smiling.

"Mom, don't cry." Sara wrapped her arms around her mother.

"It's just that you look so beautiful and it is wasted on a contract marriage," her mother whispered so that Mariam and Mrs. Tadros would not hear.

"I know Mom, but I have lived with him for a month now. He is okay. Please do not worry about me."

Her mother held her by the shoulders and nodded. "You are a strong girl. I know you will be okay." She smiled and wiped her tears.

"Let's get going," Mrs. Tadros said. "You look so amazing."

"My work is complete," added Mariam.

Sara and the others laughed. Sara hoped so because she was sick of all these lessons.

The wedding was being held in the back gardens. It was quite intimate and only a few people had been invited. Sara walked on the red carpet that had been laid on the grass, creating the aisle. The guests rose from their seats and watched Sara walking with her mother. Since her father was no more and she did not have a brother, it was her mother who was walking her down the aisle.

Her mother was dressed in her stunning mother of the bride outfit. She wore an ivory knee dress with a gold band cutting off the mid-section. She wore a golden bolero jacket with a matching hat.

Sara stared ahead and made eye contact with Raphael. He was wearing a white sherwani with silver embroidery on the collar and down the chest. He wore white trousers. His hair was cut short in the back and on the sides, with a side parting. Sara almost stopped walking. Raphael looked so good. It felt like a dream, the fact that she was getting married, and to this Adonis.

Raphael grunted. He stared down at the woman walking down the aisle. He almost could not recognize her. She was the most beautiful woman he had ever laid eyes on. He did not understand how he had not seen just how gorgeous she was. He felt his heart beating a little faster. It was weird, it had never happened before.

Sara's mother stopped walking Sara halfway down the aisle. Sara walked the rest of the way alone. Raphael and Sara maintained eye contact until she had approached him at the altar. Neither one of them said anything. They just stared at each other.

"You may be seated," the pastor said to the guests. There were less than fifty guests. Sara and Raphael had only invited close friends and family.

The guests sat down and the ceremony began. As the pastor carried out the ceremony, so many thoughts rushed through Sara's mind. She knew that she was getting married and her life was going to change. It worried her so much, but on the bright side, she was going to receive a cash incentive that day. It was going to be her first payment for contract, and it was a hefty incentive. It made her seem materialistic but she was sending that money to her mother. That money was going to be enough to look after her sisters, also. Sara was also worried about having to perform wifely duties. Raphael's family was going to want to see her and do things with her.

Raphael recited his vows and then slipped the wedding band onto Sara's finger. Sara also did the same to Raphael.

"You may kiss the bride," said the pastor. Raphael leaned in and pressed a small kiss on Sara's lips. She was shy about kissing him in front of everyone. She was shy about kissing him because they had only kissed once. Fortunately, the kiss lasted for just a second. Last time they had kissed, she had gotten so aroused. The guests rose to their feet and cheered.

The wedding reception was held outside in the courtyard. It was Sara's first time in that part of Raphael's home. The courtyard was big but not too big. There were tables and chairs set out for the guests. There was a high table only for Raphael and Sara.

Before Sara could get comfortable and stuff her face with Arabic food, she and Raphael had to have their first dance. That was something that she had not been looking forward to. Raphael wrapped one arm around Sara's small waist and pulled her closer to him. She placed one hand on his shoulder and the other in his free hand.

"Try not to mess up," he whispered to her.

"I am actually good at dancing believe it or not," she said.

Raphael raised his eyebrows.

"I do believe it."

Sara did not see that coming. The music started playing. The two of them started dancing. Being that close to Raphael made Sara's heart beat fast. She felt her stomach knot up. The combination of their bodies swaying against each other, his scent and his intense stare drove her crazy. She grew more and more aroused. She found herself wanting him to kiss her.

"You look gorgeous," he whispered in her ear. Sara widened her eyes. She did not expect him to say that. He had never paid her a complement.

"Do I really?"

"You do. The things I want to do to you right now."

"Raphael!" Sara started getting shy. What on earth was he thinking? There were people around.

Some of the guests started ululating and clapping, Sara realized that they were in front of people. She had gone into a zone where it felt as though it was only she and Raphael in the room.

**

For the reason that there would speculation about their wedding night, Sara had to be with Raphael in his chambers. He did not want gossip amongst the maids. That was how stories were leaked. Sara did not care too much, she just wanted to take her shoes off and rest, it had had been a long day.

She walked into Raphael's bedroom, which was much bigger than hers, and just kicked her shoes off. She was dying to get out of her wedding dress and just relax. That did not look like it was going to be hard. Raphael's four-poster bed was large enough to fit ten bodies.

"I am so exhausted," Sara complained to Raphael.

"We are to share the chambers and not the bed," he replied. "So you are to make your way to the sofa."

"What?"

Raphael laughed a little. "Relax. There is plenty of room here, for us both." He stopped smiling and held Sara's waist. She raised her eyebrows.

"Raphael?" She was confused. He looked at her with a lascivious glare. He pulled her closer to him so that their bodies were touching.

"I want to undress you." His voice was so deep and alluring.

"You want to do what?" Sara did not know else to say. He was so direct. He started fumbling with the back of the dress.

"You said I knew nothing about women. Tonight I will show you."

Sara giggled. "Oh you will? Like, when you said so much crap to my mother about us. You are talking crap now again." She gasped when she felt the dress coming undone.

"I do not talk crap." Raphael unclipped her veil and threw it on the floor. Sara could not believe that she was allowing him to undress her.

It did not take him long to free her from her dress. He then stood there for a moment, just looking at her and admiring her body. He dipped his head and started kissing her. This kiss was different to the last one. It was more hungry and passionate. He broke off the kiss and gently bit her earlobe.

"I want to touch you," he whispered, clearly getting aroused.

The Final Chapter

Sara let out a small moan. "Touch me then." She was already almost naked and in his arms. Raphael trailed kisses from her neck to her breasts. He caressed her back and unclipped her bra. He groaned at the sight of her naked full breasts resting on his chest.

He cupped her breasts and kissed her dark brown erect nipples. Sara held onto his stone hard arms and let him kiss her. He had not touched her that long before she was just ready for him to make love to her. He carried her to the bed and laid her down.

Raphael stared at her as he unbuttoned his sherwani. Sara felt shy because of the way he was looking at her. She knew that he wanted her; the evidence was there in his pants pointing at her. Sara gasped at the sight of his bare chest. He was ripped. She could not wait to get her hands on him.

She covered her face with her hands when he took his pants off. "So now you are suddenly shy?" he asked her. Sara giggled.

"In this situation, yes I am," she replied.

Raphael got on top of her and started kissing her. He took his time kissing every inch of her skin. He paid each attention to each spot. Sara's knees shook from the pleasure. She could feel the tension in her body building up.

He took her lace underwear off. Sara was suddenly glad that the glam squad Mariam had brought for her had forced her to wax. They wanted to wax for her but she refused. She preferred to wax herself down there than for someone else to do so. Now that

Raphael was caressing her there, she was glad that she was kempt.

"So you do not brush your hair but you shave yourself." He said to her.

"Ah, what?" Sara answered. She let out another moan and curled her toes. He slipped his finger inside of her and stroked her walls.

"Or did you shave especially for me?"

"Ah!" Sara could hardly manage anything more than that. She was too aroused and could barely concentrate on a conversation. Raphael pulled his fingers out.

"Not yet." He replaced his fingers with his male member. Sara's eyes flew open.

"Oh my." He was much bigger than she had anticipated. Fortunately, he started slowly and gently. He took his time with her and quickened the rhythm. Sara's body had never known so much pleasure.

Raphael took her to a state of euphoria. A state she had never experienced or understood. "Raphael." She moaned out his name as he touched her female parts while he made love to her. The combination was driving her insane with ecstasy. She arched her back and held onto his arms tightly. Raphael groaned and went in even deeper.

**

The next morning, Sara and Raphael woke up together. Sara expected to feel awkward about the previous night but she did not. She and Raphael were up early and just started talking. Their conversation was not an argument for once. They were just talking about random things. Raphael got out of bed.

"Where are you going?" Sara asked him.

"To shower before breakfast," he said. "Join me."

Sara sat up and used one of the sheets to cover her body. Raphael started laughing. "I have already seen you nude. So why are you covering yourself?" he asked her.

"Because," Sara laughed. She was still shy but she did not want to let him know. Raphael stared at the bed. He noticed some kind of staining on the sheets. He looked at Sara.

"You were a virgin," he said to her. Sara's eyes raced. She saw the blood on the sheets. She immediately felt shy. She just wanted the ground to open up and swallow her. "Why did you not tell me?"

"Why would I?" *How would she bring that into a conversation anyway? Hey, Raphael, I am a virgin? That was ridiculous.*

"But we just, I just, you should have told me or stopped me."

Sara looked at him. "It was my decision. I would never do what I did not want to do, so don't worry about it," she said. She had managed not to sleep with anyone else in the past. So why did Raphael feel that it was on him?

"Are you sure you will not regret this?"

"No."

Raphael took her hand and kissed it. "Okay, if you're sure," he said. He leaned in and kissed her. He carried her off to the shower.

Sara felt a little weird having breakfast with her mother and sisters and Raphael. Her mother was studying her. "Something has changed," Her mother pointed out. Sara felt even more awkward about the situation. It seems that her mother knew what she and Raphael had been doing.

"Nothing has changed," Sara replied. Elizabeth and Elaine just spoke to each other as they ate. They were still excited about the wedding. Malik frantically walked in with the newspaper. Raphael raised his eyebrows.

"Is there something wrong?" Raphael asked Malik.

"Yes, Sheikh, look at this." Malik gave him the newspaper. He looked at Sara. "I apologize, Mrs. Tadros for the interruption," he said to her.

Sara raised her eyebrows. Mrs. Tadros? It was going to be weird being called that.

"Raphael, what's wrong?" Sara asked her husband. She could see from his face that it was not good news.

"Hosny," he said with a tone of resentment.

"We have to address this," said Malik.

Sara took the newspaper from Raphael and looked at it. There was a story about Raphael's past lover. Sara frowned as she read the article. It stated that she had claimed that Raphael was not the type to get married. The story also speculated about his engagement to Sara.

"Is this the only thing?" Raphael asked.

"No, Hosny has a meeting with a Jordanian sheikh."

Raphael rose to his feet. "Where?" he asked.

"What is wrong with that? Raphael what is happening?" Sara was curious and confused.

Raphael pressed a small kiss on her lips.

"Don't worry about anything." He looked at Sara's mother. "Please forgive my abrupt leave. I have an important matter to attend to," he said to her and left.

Sara felt a little worried. She already knew about what was happening between sheikh Hosny and Raphael. She knew that he was the one behind the article. She wondered what this meeting with the Jordanian sheikh was about.

"So there has been a development between you and Raphael," Mrs. Pierce said to Sara.

"What do you mean?" Sara asked. She took a sip of her orange juice.

"The marriage has been consummated."

Sara opened her mouth to deny it but she giggled instead. "Can we talk elsewhere?" she asked her mother. She wanted to talk to her mother where her sisters could not hear. Her mother stood up and they both left for the living room.

"I have seen the way you and that man look at each other," said Mrs. Pierce as they walked into the living room.

"I thought we were discussing last night." Sara was feeling confused.

"Well, I already know that you had your wedding night. The reason that happened is because you have feelings for him."

"What?"

"At first I thought this entire thing was ridiculous. When I came for this wedding, I was intending on dragging you back to Dallas."

Sara laughed. "So what happened?" she asked.

"You both wanted to have the wedding, and at dinner I saw the way he was looking at you."

"Like what?"

"I know love when I see it."

Sara narrowed her gaze at her mother. What had the chef mixed in her naan bread? Sara had no feelings for Raphael. Yes, he was crazy attractive and responsible, but strangely, there was a caring side to him but there were no feelings involved. She did not like him, and the fact that her mother had said love? That was crazy.

"Mother, there is no love."

Her mother smiled and rubbed her cheeks.

"You are even glowing. Let me know in a few months."

*

Sara went to Raphael's chambers to check up on him. It had been a crazy week for the two of them. The media had been hounding them about the rumors that had come out. There had been so much speculation about their sudden engagement. Sara could not even turn to her mother because she and the twins had returned to Dallas.

"What are you doing?" Sara asked Raphael as she walked into his bedroom. He was just sitting at the edge of the bed looking at the tablet.

"This issue with the Jordanian Sheikh." Raphael grunted. Sara took the tablet and put it on the nightstand.

"What happened?" Sara stood between his legs and wrapped her arms around his neck. He looked at her.

"The Jordanian sheikh has been trying to buy shares in the company. So if he did, he would sell them to Hosny."

"He wants controlling shares?" Sara shook her head. "He is relentless."

"He is." Raphael buried his head in her chest. Sara kissed his forehead.

"But who was selling their shares?"

"Sheikh Salem. Fortunately, someone else purchased them." Raphael sighed. "I am sure this is not how you wanted to start your marriage."

Sara laughed. "This is not a normal marriage."

Raphael kissed her chest. He laughed a little. "Indeed."

"Laughing suits you. You should laugh more."

Raphael grunted. "How are the twins?" he asked.

"They're fine. They ask about you."

Raphael smiled. "They're so cute."

That night Sara slept in Raphael's bed. They were not making love or anything. She was just sleeping next to him peacefully. It was so strange to Raphael. She was the first woman to be in his bed. His past lovers had never come to his home. Even when they made love, he never allowed them to spend the night.

It was nice to have Sara there with him. Everything had changed for him when he saw her walking down the aisle. He realized how beautiful she was. She was also very spirited and witty. He was not sure that he was going to be able to let her go after six months. He leaned down and kissed her on the forehead. He pulled her closer to him and held her in his arms. He held his wife in his hands.

**

The next day, at the board meeting, the sheikhs gathered. They needed to appoint a new CEO. The lawyer had contracts ready. All the sheikhs had to vote for the new CEO. Raphael would have automatically won the position if Hosny had not put up so much of a fight. He even blackmailed and paid off some members of the board to side with him on the matter. After the sheikhs had voted, they were tied.

Malik walked into the conference room. "Excuse me, but the new shareholder has arrived."

The other sheikhs looked at each other in confusion. They knew that Sheikh Salem had sold his shares but they did not know who bought them.

Raphael crossed his eyebrows when Sara walked in, dressed in a blue pantsuit and a white blouse. "My apologies for being late," she said before she sat down.

"What is the meaning of this?" Hosny asked.

"Mrs. Tadros is the new shareholder," said Malik.

"Impossible!"

Sara pulled out the paperwork and showed it to Hosny. He shook his head in frustration. The paperwork was legit. So Sara was the last one left to vote. Her vote was the tie breaker. Raphael stared at her, wondering how it had happened. Sara voted for Raphael to be the CEO.

"This is not right!" Hosny protested.

"Sheikh Raphael Tadros is the new CEO of Salam Oils & Gasses," said the lawyer. Some sheikhs cheered happily, the ones that had voted for Raphael.

"If you would just sign here and here," the company lawyer said to Raphael. He signed the designated area. The other sheikhs also signed the contract. Sheikh Hosny was last to sign. His disapproval was too obvious.

"Congratulations, Sheikh Raphael Tadros. You are now the CEO of the Salam Oils & Gasses," the lawyer said to him and shook his hand. The other sheikhs also congratulated him and shook his hand.

"This is not over," Hosny said before he left. All the sheikhs left, except for Raphael. He stayed behind to talk to Sara.

"Congratulations," she said to him.

"How did you buy those shares?" he asked her. He was eager to know.

"I just met with the sheikh and purchased them."

"When?"

"Two days after the wedding."

"Where did you get the money from?"

"The money you gave me."

Raphael was shocked. Instead of spending the money he had given her, honoring their contract, she purchased the company shares instead.

"You used the money for that?" he asked.

"Yes, I bought the shares so that I could help you. As we speak they are being transferred to you."

Now Raphael was even more confused. "What do you mean?"

"I only bought them to give to you. I don't need them. They have already served my purpose." She had helped him to be the CEO by being his wife and purchasing the shares. He was so pleased to have her on his side. He took her hands into his and kissed them.

"You are an amazing woman and you deserve better."

"What do you mean?"

"From now on, the contract is void. You are free to go back to Dallas."

Sara raised her eyebrows. "And if I don't want to?"

"You would stay here with me? Why?""This is why I said that you did not know about women." Sara shook her head.

"Because I love you," she shouted.

Raphael stared at her with a blank facial expression.

"Because you love me? How can you love me?"

"I don't know but I do."

"Good, because I just might feel the same," he said. Sara frowned and started laughing. "Woman, I am serious!"

"What does that mean? I just might feel the same?"

He cleared his throat. "It means I love you," he said quietly.

"I did not hear you, please say that again?" Sara asked, pretending she did not hear him.

"Damnit, Sara Pierce, I said I love you!" he said louder. Sara giggled and wrapped her arms around him.

"Now that wasn't so hard." She smiled and kissed him.

Epilogue

Sara and Raphael galloped into the cool breeze. It was Sara's first time horseback riding. Raphael had taken her for a ride. For once, he had decided to relax during the weekend. He had always worked on weekends. He did not mind taking the weekend off to spend some time with Sara. It was crazy to him that the woman who fell in his arms in Dallas was the woman to whom he gave his heart. The marriage was meant to be a contract marriage, nothing more than business. He unexpectedly fell in love with her. He wanted to devote himself to be the best husband he could be to her.

They stopped at the top of a hill to watch the sunset. "I have never watched a sunset,." said Sara as she looked at the peach and grey skies.

"It's beautiful isn't it?" Raphael asked her.

"It is." Sara laughed. "Months ago, I was not the girl that looked at sunsets."

Raphael pulled her closer to him and held her tighter. Her back rested on his hard chest. He pressed a kiss against her neck.

"Raphael, if we fall off this horse." Sara giggled.

"Well, I am holding the reigns. It is you who will fall."

"Self-preservation, wow. How gentlemanly of you."

Raphael laughed and kissed her neck again. Sara felt perfectly happy. For once, everything in her life was going well. She had unexpectedly met the love of her life. It hadn't been the most conventional way of falling in love but then again nothing about her life had ever been conventional.

Her mother was in remission. Raphael had paid for all of her medical expenses. He had gotten her a new and bigger house. The twins had been put into a private school. Raphael was now the CEO of Salam Organization and of the oil & gasses company. She felt proud of herself that she had helped him achieve that.

The rumors about Raphael's past had been squashed with all the news about him being the CEO and the pictures of him and Sara. They were spotted together in public on my many occasions. They looked all loved up, like newlyweds.

Sara had always been a responsible and logical woman. The one time she impulsively married a sheikh for money, something that was completely out of her character, it turned out to be the best decision she had ever made.

THE END

Authors Personal Message:

Heyyyy!

I really hope you enjoyed my books and I would really love if you could give this package a rating on the store!

If you are interested in checking out all my other releases then you can see them all here on my Amazon page!

A MUST HAVE!

TALL, WHITE & ALPHA

10 BILLIONAIRE ROMANCE BOOKS BOXSET

An amazing chance to own 10 complete books for one LOW price!

This package features some of the biggest selling authors from the world of Billionaire Romance. They have collaborated to bring you this super-sized portion of love, sex and romance involving loveable heroines and Tall, White and Alpha Billionaire men.

1 The Billionaire's Designer Bride – Alexis Gold
2 The Prettiest Woman – Lena Skye
3 How To Marry A Billionaire – Susan Westwood
4 Seduced By The Italian Billionaire – CJ Howard
5 The Cowboy Billionaire's Proposal – Monica Castle
6 Seduced By The Secret Billionaire – Cherry Kay
7 Billionaire Impossible – Lacey Legend
8 Matched With The British Billionaire – Kimmy Love
9 The Billionaire's Baby Mama – Tasha Blue
10 The Billionaire's Arranged Marriage – CJ Howard

START READING THIS NOW AT THE

BELOW LINKS

Amazon.com > http://www.amazon.com/Tall-White-Alpha-Billionaire-Collection-ebook/dp/B0115KNSMA/

Amazon.co.uk > http://www.amazon.co.uk/Tall-White-Alpha-Billionaire-Collection-ebook/dp/B0115KNSMA/

Amazon.ca > http://www.amazon.ca/Tall-White-Alpha-Billionaire-Collection-ebook/dp/B0115KNSMA/

Amazon.com.au > http://www.amazon.com.au/Tall-White-Alpha-Billionaire-Collection-ebook/dp/B0115KNSMA/